A TREACHEROUS TIDE

READ ALL THE MYSTERIES IN THE
HARDY BOYS ADVENTURES:

#1 *Secret of the Red Arrow*

#2 *Mystery of the Phantom Heist*

#3 *The Vanishing Game*

#4 *Into Thin Air*

#5 *Peril at Granite Peak*

#6 *The Battle of Bayport*

#7 *Shadows at Predator Reef*

#8 *Deception on the Set*

#9 *The Curse of the Ancient Emerald*

#10 *Tunnel of Secrets*

#11 *Showdown at Widow Creek*

#12 *The Madman of Black Bear Mountain*

#13 *Bound for Danger*

#14 *Attack of the Bayport Beast*

#15 *A Con Artist in Paris*

#16 *Stolen Identity*

#17 *The Gray Hunter's Revenge*

#18 *The Disappearance*

#19 *Dungeons & Detectives*

#20 *Return to Black Bear Mountain*

COMING SOON:

#22 *Trouble Island*

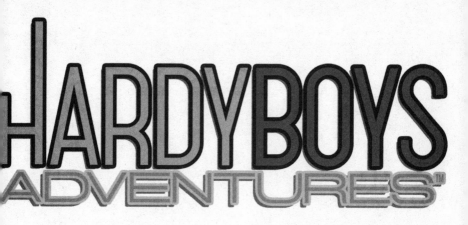

HARDY BOYS ADVENTURES™

#21 *A TREACHEROUS TIDE*

FRANKLIN W. DIXON

ALADDIN   New York London Toronto Sydney New Delhi

ALADDIN
An imprint of Simon & Schuster Children's Publishing Division
1230 Avenue of the Americas, New York, NY 10020
First Aladdin hardcover edition June 2020
Text © 2020 by Simon & Schuster, Inc.
Jacket illustration © 2020 by Kevin Keele
THE HARDY BOYS MYSTERY STORIES, HARDY BOYS ADVENTURES,
and related logos are trademarks of Simon & Schuster, Inc.
Also available in an Aladdin paperback edition.
All rights reserved, including the right of reproduction in whole or in part in any form.
ALADDIN and related logo are registered trademarks of Simon & Schuster, Inc.
For information about special discounts for bulk purchases, please contact Simon & Schuster
Special Sales at 1-866-506-1949 or business@simonandschuster.com.
The Simon & Schuster Speakers Bureau can bring authors to your live event.
For more information or to book an event contact the Simon & Schuster Speakers Bureau
at 1-866-248-3049 or visit our website at www.simonspeakers.com.
Series design by Karin Paprocki
Interior design by Mike Rosamilia
The text of this book was set in Adobe Carlson Pro.
Manufactured in the United States of America 0520 BVG
2 4 6 8 10 9 7 5 3 1
This book has been cataloged with the Library of Congress.
ISBN 978-1-5344-4137-8 (hc)
ISBN 978-1-5344-4136-1 (pbk)
ISBN 978-1-5344-4138-5 (ebook)

CONTENTS

Chapter 1	Shark!	1
Chapter 2	GONEEE	9
Chapter 3	Local Politics	18
Chapter 4	Proof Negative	29
Chapter 5	Town vs. Shark	35
Chapter 6	No Guts, No Glory	48
Chapter 7	Rare Fish	54
Chapter 8	Don't Fake the Funk	66
Chapter 9	Once Bitten	73
Chapter 10	Framed	87
Chapter 11	Cut Loose	98
Chapter 12	Beacon of Doom	108
Chapter 13	Ambush Hunters	117
Chapter 14	Downward Spiral	125
Chapter 15	Too Many Captains in the Kitchen	130
Chapter 16	The Final Plunge	146
Chapter 17	Catch of the Day	152

SHARK! 1

FRANK

I STOOD ATOP THE CLEAR, AQUA-COLORED WATER, the gentle current lapping at the edges of my stand-up paddleboard as a warm island breeze tickled my cheeks.

"This is the life." I sighed, letting the long paddle rest idly in the water while our group waited for the woman paddling toward us from the sixty-five-foot research vessel anchored a hundred yards offshore from Lookout Key, a tiny island in the middle of the Florida Keys archipelago.

"I tell myself the same thing every day," the man on the paddleboard to my right replied, absently rubbing a tan bicep tattooed with a picture of a majestic shark gliding over a ship's anchor. Below it was the name *Sally*, which also happened to be the name painted on the hull of the boat offshore. It wasn't a coincidence. Captain Rogers—or "Cap" as he'd said to call him when he'd picked us up from the airport earlier that day—was the R/V *Sally*'s captain. R/V stood for "research vessel," and it was one of the main reasons we were there.

"It'll get even better once we get you kids introduced to some of our friendly neighborhood sharks," Cap added, pushing his sun-bleached blond hair off his forehead. "We don't normally get too many of the really big boys and girls in the coastal area we'll be surveying, but there have been a couple nice-size tiger sharks spotted. With a little luck, we'll be able to get one on board the R/V to study while you're here."

"I'm still not so sure about the sharks part of this trip, but I could definitely get used to the scenery," a red-haired girl my age said with a little shudder. Abby was one of the other two Bayport Aquarium student volunteers besides Joe and me who'd signed up for the Oceanic Explorers Exchange Program with the Lookout Shark Lab, which used the R/V as its floating base.

I breathed in the salty air and smiled. I was sure about both the sharks *and* the scenery. It wasn't like I hadn't been in the Atlantic Ocean before, but all the palm trees and pelicans made this practically another world compared to our hometown of Bayport up north. The Florida Keys are over a thousand miles south and a whole lot more tropical. We might not have been on vacation, but the built-in vacay vibes didn't hurt.

"So, um, how big *are* those tiger sharks you mentioned?" a kid named Randy, the fourth volunteer, asked timidly.

"Don't worry, we haven't lost a student yet." Cap laughed. "In fact, one of the main goals of our research is to let people know about the importance of sharks. They're not the villainous monsters the movies make them out to be."

"Did you know you're statistically more likely to be attacked by a cow than by a shark?" I said, trying to reassure Randy. To be totally honest, I was kind of trying to reassure myself, too. I mean, I believed a hundred percent in the lab's mission and was super excited to get hands-on shark ecology experience. Still, it was hard not to be a little nervous around predators with such a fearsome reputation.

"Yeah, but we're not going to be swimming with cows," Abby reminded me.

I was just about to reply with another reassuring fact when I felt something bump the underside of my board. It wasn't until it clamped down on my ankle that I screamed.

My board rocked beneath my feet, sending me splashing into the ocean, where whatever horror lurked below was waiting.

The creature that burst through the water beside me wasn't a shark, though. It was my younger brother, Joe!

"Hardy shark!" he cackled. "The awesomest and most mysterious shark of all!"

"Very funny," I grumbled, but even with my heart beating out of my chest, I couldn't help smiling.

I didn't know about "awesomest," but Joe had the mysterious part right. Or mystery-*solving*, at least. Joe and I had well-earned reputations as Bayport's foremost teenage private eyes. We weren't on this trip to detect, though. Not that a case involving a shark would be our first—we'd had a run-in with a pair of them when someone kidnapped an endangered sea turtle from the Bayport Aquarium a while back. The only mysteries we expected to find in the Florida Keys on this trip were mysteries of the deep!

Everyone was still laughing as I climbed back onto my paddleboard, even Cap.

"Get the horseplay out of your systems now, kids." I looked up to see that the woman who'd been approaching us from the research vessel was now bobbing alongside us on her paddleboard. She was middle-aged and wore board shorts and a Lookout Shark Lab T-Shirt. Her shirt wasn't the only shark-themed item she was wearing. A braided leather necklace with a shark's tooth pendant hung around her neck. Her paddleboard stood out too. It had a vintage feel—a bright-blue-and-green paint job with wave patterns running around the edges.

This was the first time I'd seen E. Ella Edwards, PhD, in person, but I recognized her from the video meet and greet before the trip. Dr. Edwards was the head of Shark Lab, and one of the world's most renowned marine biologists.

"I want you to have fun on this trip, but oceanic research is serious business. If you mess around like this on the R/V, someone could get seriously hurt." She glared at each of us, Cap included, with clear, blue-green eyes that matched the water.

"Sorry, Triple E," Cap mumbled.

"Sorry, Dr. Edwards," Joe added.

"I'm not just talking about people getting hurt," she added. "We'll be handling live sharks, and if we're not careful, they can also be harmed. Global shark populations are declining rapidly, and we can't afford to lose any because you're goofing around."

Everyone nodded in solemn agreement. A big part of why we'd all wanted to come on this trip was the adventure, but as aquarium volunteers, we all cared deeply about the ocean and its inhabitants, and we were here to help make a difference.

Dr. Edwards's sea-colored eyes crinkled as the stern glare turned into a broad smile. "You can call me Trip if you want—everyone else does. Or Triple E, or EEE. I have a nickname for every initial."

"You got it, Trip!" I said.

"I can't wait to get you all trained as junior members of the Shark Lab research team. When most people think about sharks, they think about *Jaws*, but great whites are one of over five hundred species, and those are only the ones we know about. Sharks aren't just the ocean's premier apex predators. They are evolutionary marvels that have survived and thrived since the time of the dinosaurs."

"Up until the last century," Cap added bleakly.

Dr. Edwards's smile faded. "A lot of people don't think the survival of creatures like sharks affects them much, but sharks are a measuring stick for the entire world's marine ecosystems."

"Without healthy oceans, millions and millions of people would go hungry, so it's our food chain that's affected too," I chimed in. Part of my job as a Bayport Aquarium volunteer was giving little kids tours of the shark exhibits, so I knew more about our finned friends than your average teenage detective. "Lots of sharks means lots of fish and a rich diversity of the sea life that provides food for a huge part of the world's population."

Trip snapped her fingers. "Bull's-eye. Healthy sharks equal a healthy ocean. Without them, the entire ecosystem starts to collapse. Theirs *and* ours."

"And it's us humans who are mostly to blame," Cap said bitterly.

"Knowledge and action can change that," Trip asserted. "Shark Lab isn't just here to help sharks; it's to help people, too."

The sky had darkened while we were talking, and a thick bank of fog had begun rolling in toward the pier to our right, obscuring the old lighthouse poking up from the peninsula farther down the coast.

Dr. Edwards held her palm out and looked up as the first drops of rain began to fall. "I'd hoped to start your trip off with a paddleboard tour of the mangrove swamp past Alligator Lighthouse, where the lemon sharks have their nursery."

"Nothing cuter than shark pups," Cap interjected.

"Looks like the weather forecast was right, though," Dr. Edwards said. "Cap, why don't you get the kids settled onshore while I check on the pups."

There was a collective groan from me and my fellow volunteers.

Dr. Edwards gazed toward the vanishing lighthouse. "This part of the country doesn't usually get a lot of fog, but this island is a bit of its own microclimate. It's not unusual for fog to roll in this time of day now. If you're not careful, it's easy to get turned around. From the look of that sky, a nasty storm is rolling in with it."

Cap nodded in agreement. "We don't want any of you lost at sea your first night here."

"I second that," Randy said heartily.

"I'll see you all at Chuck's Shuck Shack for dinner," Dr. Edwards said as she turned her board and began paddling toward the fog.

"How come it's safe for her and not us?" Abby asked.

Cap chuckled. "No one said it was safe. But she knows her way around. Besides, Trip is fearless. Paddling out to the mangroves is her evening ritual whenever we're not out on the R/V. It takes a hurricane to keep her inside."

As we paddled for shore, I turned to look back and caught

one final glimpse of Dr. Edwards disappearing into the fog. We'd just stepped off our boards in the shallow water a few minutes later when we heard someone scream farther down the beach.

"GET OUT OF THE WATER!"

The word that followed was unmistakable.

"SHARK!"

Randy ran for the beach so fast, he tripped over his feet, tumbling face-first into the sand. Abby was right behind him.

My heart was thumping too when I remembered Joe's prank. Apparently, he wasn't the only one with a predatory sense of humor.

"Somebody's probably just messing around—" I started to say when I saw Randy pointing toward the fog, opening and closing his mouth like he was trying to say something but couldn't quite get the words out.

I followed his finger, and that's when I saw it for myself: a large gray dorsal fin slicing through the water where I'd last seen Dr. Edwards before she'd vanished into the mist.

GONEEE 2

JOE

MY FIRST THOUGHT WHEN I SAW THE dorsal fin was, *Cool!* My second thought was, *Wow, that thing's gotta belong to a really big shark.* My third thought was, *Where's EEE?*

The last time I'd looked, she'd been pretty much right where that shark was now.

I wasn't the only one wondering.

"It's going to get Dr. Edwards!" Abby called out as the last few swimmers fled the waves.

The people onshore gathered at the water's edge to gawk and take pictures of the massive fin as it dipped back below the surface. Lookout was one of the Keys' smaller inhabited islands, so the beach wasn't very crowded, but that fin had instantly attracted an audience.

"Trip will be fine. She's been in the water with sharks since before she was your age." The worried look on Cap's face didn't match his words, though. "Hard to identify it at this distance from just the dorsal, but judging by the size, that was probably one of the big tigers that's been hanging around."

"But aren't tiger sharks one of the most aggressive species?" Randy's voice cracked as he spoke. "I heard they'll eat *anything*."

I knew from all the shark factoids my older, nerdier brother, Frank, had been rambling about leading up to our trip that tiger sharks had a reputation for being the "garbage cans of the sea." Everything from tires to entire horse heads had been found in their stomachs. I also knew they could grow to be more than fifteen feet and up to two thousand pounds. There was a reason they weren't called "kitten sharks."

"They have a bad reputation, but even with the more aggressive species, attacks are still super rare," Frank offered, sounding not exactly confident as he squinted into the thickening fog.

"It's a good thing that wasn't a cow, or she'd really be in trouble," I said, trying to lighten the mood.

"Don't sharks sometimes see surfboards and paddleboards from below and think they're seals or something?" Randy whimpered.

"One out of millions and millions, maybe—" A clap of

thunder cut Cap off before he could finish. The rain followed, turning the drizzle into a full-on tropical shower that sent most of the gawkers running for cover.

An old beach bum in an open linen shirt and cutoff cargo shorts crossed the beach toward us. "You see the size of that thing, Cap? Mighta been a fifteen-footer," he called, pushing wet strands of long white hair out of his eyes. "Want me to get a boat in the water to check on Triple E?"

"She knows what she's doing, Dougie," Cap replied with less confidence than I would have liked. "I'm more worried about getting these kids out of the storm."

Dougie made a sucking sound with his teeth. "I don't know, Cap. Woulda thunk she'd have turned around and come back when all that hooting and hollering started. She shouldn't be out on that board in a thunderstorm, anyway. Been telling her that for years. She's lucky she hasn't been fried by lightning yet."

"By that reasoning, you shouldn't be out on that boat either," Cap pointed out.

Dougie grinned, exposing a cracked incisor. "They don't call me Danger Dougie for nothin'. I'm going out. You coming?"

Cap sighed. "Might as well, so you don't get lost. Everyone knows about your sense of direction. You kids get on up to the pier and out of the storm. Get yourselves some Key-lada smoothies and pink shrimp poppers at Chuck's Shuck Shack while you wait. I'll join you there."

"Pink shrimps are a local speciality," Dougie said.

Cap put a hand on my shoulder and gave me a gentle push toward the pier. "Just tell Chuck it's on me. I've got a tab open."

Dougie made that sucking sound with his teeth again. "Don't we all."

"We're wasting our time, Doug. We'll be lucky if Trip doesn't bite *our* heads off for trying to tell her what to do. She'll be fine on her—"

That was when a woman's scream echoed through the fog.

Everything went silent again except for the pounding of the rain.

Cap looked at Dougie. "Get the boat. I'm right behind you."

Dougie took off for the marina at a run.

Turning back to us, Cap forced a smile. "The shark probably just scared her. I'm sure she's fine."

His words sounded hollow. He'd just finished telling us how fearless EEE was. If she'd screamed like that, there had to be a reason.

"We're coming with you," I volunteered automatically. Frank gulped, but nodded. We might not have been on a case, but if someone was in danger, we were going to try to help them if we could.

"Sorry, Joe. I don't think the Bayport Aquarium would forgive us if we got its volunteers struck by lightning. Go up to Chuck's and get dry. I'll be back soon."

Abby and Randy didn't have to be told again. They took off running for the palm-frond-covered awning of the restaurant at the inland end of the pier. Frank and I reluctantly followed them, occasionally glancing back to watch Cap and Dougie as they headed for the marina.

Chuck's Shuck Shack was perfectly positioned to give anybody sitting outside under the awning or by the open windows a clear view of both the beach to the left and the marina on the other side. I looked back across the sand one last time and saw a small fishing boat heading into the fog. The storm had picked up, turning into a real downpour that made it all but impossible to identify the two figures I knew were Danger Dougie and Cap on its deck.

When we stepped through the door, it was obvious we hadn't been the only ones to see the dorsal fin. Whispers of "fin," "shark," and "man-eater" rose from some of the tables. Abby waved to us from a table near the window, where she was sitting with Randy.

Sharks weren't just the talk of the restaurant. The walls were jam-packed with fishing pictures and mounted trophies among nets and oars and all kinds of other nautical tchotchkes.

As we walked in, a short-haired woman with big brown eyes in her midtwenties looked up from drying glasses behind the bar.

"How can I help you boys?" she asked with a smile.

"We'll take two Key-ladas and your biggest basket of

shrimp poppers, please," I said, my stomach suddenly rumbling louder than the thunder. I eyed the specials board over the bar. "Throw in the pickled red herring tacos, too."

The woman nodded approvingly. "Good choice. Go ahead and grab a table, and we'll bring everything out to you."

"Is Chuck here? Cap said to tell him to put our food on his tab," Frank said.

"Oh, he did, did he?" The woman grinned and turned to a guy in a panama hat chowing down on a basket of calamari at the end of the bar. "Hey, Ron? Is Chuck here?"

"That depends. You gonna cover my tab for me if'n I say no?" the guy asked.

"Ha! The way you cleaned me out with that straight flush last week, I practically already am."

"Worth a try." He shrugged. "You're looking at her, boys."

"You're Chuck?" I blurted. As a detective, I should have known that making assumptions is a good way to get yourself in trouble, but it hadn't occurred to me that Chuck might not be a dude.

"Chuck Junior, to be more precise." She pointed to a framed picture over the bar of a grinning man with a bushy beard wearing a beat-up canvas cap. Even with the beard, the big brown eyes were a dead giveaway that they were related. Below the picture was a plaque that read CHUCK ADAMS, MAY HE FISH IN PEACE. "My birth certificate says

Charlotte, if you want to get technical about it, but the locals would have revolted if I changed the name on the sign when I inherited the place."

A barefoot woman in a long yellow raincoat pushed open the door and threw back her hood. "Chuck, you hear about the shark?"

"Only ten times in the last ten minutes."

The woman whistled. "You shoulda seen the size of that fin. Coulda been a twenty-footer, easy."

"Twenty? It was twenty-five, at least!" Ron weighed in through a mouthful of fried squid.

"Sure it was, just like that grouper you had on the line last week." Chuck rolled her eyes and turned back to Frank and me. "You know that old cliché about fishermen always exaggerating? It's true. Ron was in the little boys' room when that shark swam by. He didn't even see it."

The guy waved her away. "Well, however big it was, I don't like it prowling around that close to shore. My kids go swimming at that beach."

"Sharks have been swimming these beaches a lot longer than any of us," Chuck said. "The way I figure it, we're the ones dipping our toes into *their* turf. They have as much of a right to be here as we do."

Ron harrumphed and went back to his calamari. "I'm with Maxwell on this one."

This time, it was Chuck who waved Ron away. I didn't know who Maxwell was, but Chuck didn't seem impressed.

"Trip and Cap really brought me around on the shark conservation thing. They're some of the coolest creatures on the planet. Sure would be a shame if they weren't around anymore. Any sharks you see on the wall are from the old days. I even pulled the mako steaks from the menu. Everything at Chuck's is local, wild, and sustainable. Like me."

"You're wild, all right. I can't believe you still say that stuff after what happened to your pops," Ron grumbled.

Frank jumped in before I could ask what he meant. "You're not worried about Dr. Edwards?" my brother asked Chuck as another crack of thunder rumbled over the island.

"I'm not worried about the shark or the storm. Trip is practically part shark herself. She'll be fine."

Cap had said the same thing, but unlike the R/V captain, Chuck didn't appear to have a hint of doubt.

Her confidence seemed a bit strange, and it wasn't until Frank and I exchanged a confused glance that it dawned on me why. It had only been after the downpour started and the beach cleared out that we heard the scream. The most alarming part of the day's shark tale hadn't reached the Shuck Shack yet.

"We heard a woman scream a few minutes after the fin vanished," I said, leveling with Chuck. "We didn't see Dr. Edwards or the shark again."

I could see Chuck's confidence waver. "You sure it was her? Not just some hysterical lookie-loo?"

"I guess it could have been someone else, but it definitely

came from the water inside the fog, not from the shore," Frank replied. "Cap and Dougie took a boat out looking for her."

Chuck was silent for a minute as she stared out the open windows into the storm.

"I'll have your food brought out when it's ready," she said absently, stepping out from behind the bar and heading toward the kitchen. When I looked back, she was on the phone with someone, having what looked like an intense conversation.

Frank and I grabbed seats by the window, near Abby and Randy's table, where we could see the water. A waiter showed up with our food a few minutes later. In the meantime, Chuck must have spread the word about the scream, because the buzz around the restaurant shot up a few notches. It grew even louder as more people arrived. It looked like Chuck's Shuck Shack was the center of the Lookout Key universe, and all anyone wanted to talk about now was EEE and the shark.

By the time Cap stumbled in a little while later, the crowd had worked itself into a frenzy. He locked eyes with Chuck first.

"We made it to the mangroves but had to turn back when the storm picked up. Trip—" Cap rubbed a hand down his still-wet face. He looked shell-shocked. "She's gone."

LOCAL POLITICS
3

FRANK

"WHAT DO YOU MEAN, GONE?" CHUCK demanded.

"There's no sign of her. Her board, either. It's like she vanished." Cap looked helplessly at his feet. "Dougie radioed the coast guard, but there are major storm warnings in effect, and they can't launch a search until morning."

Chuck narrowed her eyes. "They won't be the only ones searching. I'll make sure half the town is out there looking along with them."

"Not me," Randy announced from behind us. "I'm not taking another step near the water as long as there's a marine-biologist-eating shark around. The only place I'm going is home."

Abby nodded vigorously. "We discussed it, and Randy and I are getting on the first flight back to Bayport."

"That's probably for the best." Cap sighed heavily. "We're not going to be able to do the research we had planned, and Trip isn't here to lead you."

I didn't even have to look at my brother to know we were on the same page. We'd suddenly found ourselves in the middle of a missing persons case, and the prime suspect was a shark. There was no way we were going back to Bayport now.

"We're staying to help you find Dr. Edwards," I said.

Cap put a sympathetic hand on my shoulder. "I appreciate the sentiment, guys, but there's really nothing you can do."

"Oh, you'd be surprised," Joe replied. "Our suspects usually have legs instead of fins, but this isn't our first missing persons investigation."

"Marine biology is just a sideline," I explained. "Our real hobby is private detection."

Chuck rubbed her chin while she contemplated the idea. "Huh. Well, consider yourselves hired. I can pay you in shrimp."

"Deal!" Joe enthusiastically shook Chuck's hand. "We would have done it for free, but we'll definitely do it for free food!"

"Joe can eat a lot of shrimp," I warned her.

She smiled. "I'll take my chances."

Cap eyed us skeptically. "Teenage private eyes? They're only kids, Chuck."

"So was I when I started running this place. We need all the help we can get. Hopefully, Triple E just got blown off course in the storm and took shelter somewhere down the coast, but she's a friend, and I want all hands on deck until she's back safe."

Cap didn't seem entirely convinced, but he looked too drained to argue.

"I was thinking we could go up to the top of the lighthouse with binoculars first thing in the morning to get a bird's-eye view of the entire coastline," I said.

"It's a good thought, but that place is abandoned for a reason," Cap warned. "It's basically a death trap with a broken light on top. The town condemned it years ago. You boys go in there, and we'll probably find ourselves looking for three people instead of just one."

"Pretty amazing it's still standing, actually," Chuck mused. "I keep waiting to wake up one morning after one of these big storms and find it swept into the sea."

Cap scowled. "The mayor and his flunkies on the council figure nature will do the job for them eventually. Save them money on demolition."

Ron cleared his throat and aimed a piece of calamari in Cap's direction. "Maybe the town would be able to afford to do that kind of stuff if your Shark Lab wasn't so set on sinking Maxwell's new development. A lot of folks are mad about Trip saying she'd use her vote on the town council to reject it. A big, fancy resort like Mangrove Palace could have all us locals swimming in clams, what with all the jobs and tourism business and beneficial economic whatnots."

Ron pointed a thumb over his shoulder in the direction of a corner table toward the back, where a tall, well-dressed man appeared to be holding court. He had a business-tropical look in his fitted, open-collar linen shirt, with rolled-up sleeves exposing a fancy gold dive watch. Most of Chuck's customers were some combination of soggy and windswept from the storm, but the man's expensive haircut was perfectly in place. It looked like he'd just come from the stylist. And from the way people were hanging on his every word and stopping by to pay their respects, he could have passed for the local Mafia don. Cap and Chuck both eyed the guy wearily. I had a hunch that this was the Maxwell that Ron was talking about.

"Dr. Edwards is on the town council?" Joe asked.

"It's a good thing, too," Cap confirmed. "The Mangrove Palace development plan is an ecological disaster for the mangrove swamp. It threatens a whole list of species, including the lemon shark pups that nurse there. It puts the whole lemon shark population at risk, and he knows it. That's why he's trying to ram it through the council before Trip can even finish her environmental impact study."

"I'm all for Lookout Key prospering, Ron, but this resort thing is shortsighted," Chuck said. "This island is a tourist destination because of its natural beauty and sea life. You bulldoze over it to build a resort, and you're destroying one of the big things that makes us special."

Cap nodded. "Trip's vote is the only thing keeping Lookout Key from spearing itself in the foot."

"Easy for you to say, with that fancy boat of yours, but a lot of us could use the money Maxwell's promising," Ron shot back. "Some folks might even say that shark did the town a favor. Without Trip around to put the kibosh on it, sounds like the council's gonna give Maxwell the green light."

"Take that back or it's gonna be you that's battered instead of those squid," Cap snapped, balling his hands into fists.

Ron held his hands up defensively, nearly toppling off his stool in the process. "Hey, whatcha picking on me for? I said *some folks* might say that, not me. Sheesh."

"There's still no evidence Trip was even attacked by a shark," I reminded him. "Shark attacks may get a lot of press—they make a good story—but in reality, they almost never happen."

Ron looked at me like I was delusional. "Everybody saw that fin, and now the lady's gone. What more proof do you need?"

"You're mixing up proof and suspicion," Joe informed him. "Just because a suspect is seen in the neighborhood where a crime may have happened doesn't automatically mean they did it. A lot of times in missing persons cases, nothing fishy happened and the person turns up fine."

Ron didn't seem swayed by Joe's logic. "Well, I sure do hope you're right about Trip being okay. But maybe you could wait until after tomorrow's council meeting to find her? The whole town will be better off if that resort gets built. Then we'll be able to buy all the fancy new lighthouses we want!"

"The town doesn't need some big, toxic resort's money," Chuck scoffed. "With all the bribes the mayor's been pocketing for himself, the cheapskate could have easily ponied up the cash to renovate Alligator Lighthouse a few years back when it could've still been saved, and paid for a lot of other stuff around town too."

"That's pure hearsay!" a voice bellowed from the door. We turned to see a large man in an ill-fitting white linen suit. "As everyone knows, I divested myself of stock in every local business that might present a conflict of interest with my mayoral duties."

"Sure, you did, Boothby," Cap said, his voice drenched in sarcasm. "*After* the state opened an investigation into you trading political favors to beef up your business interests for personal gain."

"Lies! It's a hoax by my political enemies to distract the good people of Lookout from the real threats facing our community. Like—" Boothby paused a little too long, as if he was still trying to figure out what to say. "Like—like sharks!"

Cap's and Chuck's mouths dropped open. There was a

rumble of approval from a number of Chuck's other patrons, though. Boothby soaked it in and stood up a little taller.

"I've long been a law-and-order mayor, and it's high time the fish played by the rules too. In fact, I'm thinking of making it a cornerstone of my reelection campaign. Attacks on our citizens will not be tolerated."

"Hold your seahorses there, Mayor," Chuck cautioned. "Like my young friends said, we don't even know there was an attack. It's a lot more likely Trip got blown off course in the storm."

Boothby ignored her. "The safety of our citizens is paramount, and I won't rest until our beaches are safe again."

"Ain't the first time a paddleboarder been eaten either," Ron chimed in approvingly.

Chuck gave Ron an eye roll. "Dad wasn't eaten. The shark took a chomp out of his board, decided it wasn't a seal, and moved on."

Ron's comment earlier about something happening to Chuck Sr. suddenly made sense. Chuck's dad had been attacked by a shark too, and while paddleboarding, no less! Chuck didn't seem bothered by the possibility that something similar might have happened to EEE.

"No harm, no foul," Chuck went on. "The shark gave Dad a good scare *and* one of his all-time favorite stories. I'd say, in that encounter, he came out on top. Besides, that was, like, thirty years ago. There hasn't been a single attack on Lookout Key since."

"You see?" the mayor plowed ahead undeterred. "We've been under siege for decades!"

"Wait a second. That's not what I—" Chuck began to reply, but the mayor was on a roll.

"It's long past time we put a stop to this aggression, and I'm going to be the one who finally does something about it!" Boothby pounded his fist on the bar. "I want this shark caught! Councilwoman Edwards *will* be avenged!"

"Avenged?" Cap cried, gripping the bar so hard, his knuckles went white. "Trip is one of the Keys' biggest shark advocates! Going after them is the last thing she'd want."

Mayor Boothby snapped his fingers as if he'd just had a brilliant idea. "You can relinquish my reservation for the evening, Chuck."

"Been consulting the thesaurus again, huh, Mayor?" Chuck asked with a smirk.

If Boothby realized she was making fun of him, he didn't show it.

"I'm going to prepare an anti-shark initiative to present at the town council meeting."

The mayor turned and marched back out of the restaurant into the rain. Cap looked sick to his stomach. Between the vote on the shark-endangering resort, the mayor's new anti-shark platform, and the missing shark-loving council member, the town council meeting everyone was talking about was shaping up to be a doozy.

Chuck covered her face with her palm. "I've known

Boothby since I was a baby. He's practically family. But how this town keeps reelecting that windbag as mayor, I will never understand. I don't think he knows what half the words coming out of his mouth mean. And he doesn't even bother to learn the rules, let alone play by them!"

Joe and I sat back and watched the local drama unfold. Sometimes, a detective's best tool is simple observation. We were still getting the lay of Lookout Key's land, and the social scene at Chuck's was giving us a good primer on who was who. Hopefully, it would help us figure out who we could count on to help in our search the next morning. From the sound of it, Mayor Boothby was going to be too wrapped up in his own agenda to make the list. So much for public service!

"I think Mayor B. is onto something with this one," drawled a voice from the other end of the bar. Ron quickly scooted over to make room the second he saw the man swaggering up.

"That's right, Captain Diamond. That's right!" Ron nodded along so enthusiastically, I thought he might hurt himself. His voice quavered as he made a show of cleaning off a space at the bar. From the way he was acting, I'd say he was scared of Diamond. I'm not sure I blamed him.

The man had long, dark hair streaked with gray and tied back with a bandanna, and a thick beard, also graying. His eyebrows arched at sinister angles, and a sneer looked like it was permanently imprinted on his lips. Instead of a shirt, he had on a salt-worn leather vest festooned with nautical pins, patches, hooks, and lures. A tattooed shark hung upside down by its tail on each exposed bicep, a tiger shark on the left and a great hammerhead on the right. One forearm was adorned with a harpoon, the other a huge fishing hook. EEE had worn a shark's-tooth necklace; Diamond had an enormous bloody shark's tooth tattooed right on his chest like a permanent pendant. The overall look was basically biker pirate, and it appeared Captain Diamond had the attitude to match.

Cap's face drew into a scowl. If looks could kill, Cap's would have. I understood why when Diamond placed his hands on the bar. There was a single word tattooed on the back of each hand. Together, they read SHARK HUNTER.

Diamond smirked back at Cap, appearing unbothered by the hostility radiating from across the bar.

"I know who we can't count on to help us find Trip," Chuck muttered, throwing Diamond a side-eye glare.

"It ain't that scientist we need to be searching for. It's the monster that done snatched her outta the water," Diamond announced to the room.

"Your line's just twisted because Trip and I got you fined for catching protected hammerheads," Cap shot back.

Diamond gritted his teeth. "Seems to me sharks ain't the ones need protecting. Kinda ironic, your lady scientist friend getting gobbled up by one of her precious little guppies. Cosmic justice, if you ask me."

"No one did, and if you don't watch your mouth, you'll be hanging on your wall along with all those sharks you murdered," Cap spat, stalking toward Diamond's end of the bar.

"Bring it on, Rogers," Diamond replied, cracking the knuckles on his tattooed hands. "I'm running low on chum, and you'd make mighty tasty Jaws bait."

There were gasps and murmurs from the crowd as everyone in the restaurant stopped to watch the two men march toward each other with clenched fists.

They only made it one more step before a loud *CRACK* sounded from behind the bar. Both men froze and turned to Chuck, who was now gripping a short wooden oar.

"Knock it off, or the next thing I paddle won't be this bar top. One more step, and I'll bend you both over the bar and turn your behinds into captain fillets. You know I will too."

Apparently, they did know, because they both backed off instantly.

Diamond dropped some cash on the bar before swaggering toward the door.

"Gotta go on home and get my beauty rest, anyhow," he said with an exaggerated yawn. "Got a big day tomorrow. While y'all are wasting your time looking for your little friend, I'll be doing the hunting that really matters."

PROOF NEGATIVE

4

JOE

DIAMOND PUSHED HIS WAY PAST A spaced-out-looking gangly guy in his early twenties who didn't get out of the captain's way fast enough. The guy tumbled to the floor, muttering an apology.

I narrowed my eyes at Diamond's leather-vested back. I had to admit, he was kind of a cool-looking dude, but I can't stand bullies, and it was pretty clear the guy liked pushing people around as much as he did sharks.

"Sorry for losing my cool, Chuck." Cap massaged his temples. "That guy just does something to me."

"Hey, I don't blame you for getting heated at that sea slug. I just don't want you two killing each other in my restaurant."

Cap barked out a bitter laugh. "I'll make sure to kill him

somewhere else. The creep had at least one thing right, though. Tomorrow's a big day and I need some sleep." He turned to Frank and me. "I really appreciate you boys wanting to help, but I think it's best if you go home with your friends. This isn't what you signed up for, and I'm not going to have time to babysit you."

"We signed up to help the shark conservation effort, and right now the best way to do that is to find Dr. Edwards so she can get back to work," Frank said resolutely.

"No babysitting required. We can hold our own," I assured him.

Cap gave us both a measuring look before replying. "Meet me at the marina at four a.m. I still don't know about this detective business, but as long as you're here, I'm responsible for you, and I want the R/V on the water before sunrise."

"Aye, aye, Captain!" I said.

He looked at me sadly before walking out the door. When I turned back, the gangly guy Diamond had knocked over had squeezed up to the bar beside me.

"How you doing, Shaggy?" Chuck asked.

I gotta say, the name fit! He looked just like Shaggy from *Scooby-Doo*.

"Oh, I . . . um, nothing!" Shaggy answered nervously. He seemed about as composed as his cartoon namesake too. "I just . . . um . . . Can I get an order of pink poppers and whale fries to go?"

The back of Shaggy's T-shirt read *Scuba-Doo Dive School,*

with a cartoon of Shaggy giving a thumbs-up while scuba diving.

"Now, there's a guy who knows how to lean into his nickname," I whispered to Frank.

"You know, Shaggy from *Scooby-Doo* is kind of a fellow detective, if you think about it," Frank noted.

Our fellow-ish detective placed a bill on the bar. It was only a twenty, but Chuck looked back and forth between the bill and Shaggy like she couldn't believe her eyes.

"Shaggy paying cash for food instead of adding it to his tab? Today keeps getting weirder and weirder."

"I just, you know, had a big day at the dive school, and figured it was good luck to start settling up."

Chuck smiled warmly. "Glad to hear things are looking up for you, Shag."

She hollered the order to the waiter we'd seen earlier.

"We should probably call it a night too, Joe," Frank suggested, "Let's head back to the hotel."

"I'm with you, bro. With a four a.m. start time, we're really going to earn those shrimp."

I was about to say goodbye to Chuck when she turned around and rang a big bell behind the bar. The noisy Shuck Shack went instantly quiet.

"Wow, Chuck has her customers trained well," I quipped.

"Okay, listen up, folks!" she hollered, her hands cupped around her mouth. "We're closing early tonight. I want everyone with a boat joining the search first thing tomorrow. Let's bring Trip home!"

• • •

"I'm sorry if I was hard on you boys last night," Cap told us early the next morning as the R/V *Sally* headed south into the cloudy dawn sky. "Trip going missing like this just has me really shaken up. I really do appreciate you sticking around to help." Abby and Randy, our fellow volunteers, were heading to the airport in a few hours.

We'd left behind the familiar landmarks of Lookout Pier and Alligator Lighthouse an hour before and were slowly cruising just offshore, closely scanning the coastline. The R/V was basically a sixty-five-foot floating research station with multiple decks, a ton of cool equipment, and a full-time crew of five besides the captain. Everyone seemed to recognize that Cap wasn't in the mood for small talk, and the crew took their commands diligently, going about their jobs without bothering him.

You could tell it was a tightly run ship. Everyone seemed to know their roles and did their work efficiently. Cap's first mate, Kat (who told us to "try not to get in the way" in not the most friendly voice), was monitoring the radio to communicate with the coast guard and the other local ships participating in the search party. Every other free hand without an urgent task was on lookout duty. The fierce storm the night before had turned into more-on-than-off rain, which didn't make our job any easier. *Or* any more comfortable, although custom R/V *Sally* rain slickers helped a little. If the weather forecast was right, we were going to be getting plenty of mileage out of them—there was another big storm front on the way.

"Is there anywhere you can think Trip might try to take shelter if she did wash up onshore?" Frank asked Cap.

"In a storm like last night's? Wherever she could," he said, binoculars fixed to his eyes. "That storm got a whole lot worse a whole lot quicker than anyone expected. She knows the coastlines of the Keys as well as anyone, though, so she'd be able to find shelter if there was any. Last night's current could have carried her pretty far south, so that's the direction we'll start our search."

"If anyone can find her quickly, it's you, Cap," Frank said. "You and Trip have probably explored every inch of these waters together researching sharks, huh?"

Cap lowered the binoculars.

"I know a little something about sharks and marine biology, sure, but I'm no scientist. I just believe in what Trip and Shark Lab are doing. She supplies the brains, I supply the boat." He gave the starboard rail a squeeze and smiled down at the vessel. "I don't have kids, and *Sally* here is like my baby. We couldn't be prouder to be helping Trip and Shark Lab accomplish their mission. I can't even imagine what will happen to the research without her."

"If she's out there, we'll find her," I said as confidently as I could. It felt strange trying to reassure a real captain.

He nodded at the binoculars he'd given us both earlier. "Holler if you see anything. That includes any large dorsal fins. I'm not going to assume the worst, but like you said last night, that shark we saw is a suspect."

He stared into the mist, sighed to himself, and walked off.

"We've questioned some pretty fierce customers, but I am kinda curious to get to interrogate an actual shark," I admitted.

We were watching Cap pace the deck with his binoculars when Kat's voice called out from the main cabin. "Cap! Dougie's on the radio! He says he found something!"

Cap sprinted for the cabin, and so did we.

"Hit me," Cap commanded as he ran inside.

"Go ahead, Dougie," Kat said into the radio. "You're on with Cap."

"I was checking my lobster pots before joining the search," Dougie's voice crackled over the radio receiver. "You know, like I do every morning. And I—"

"Did you find her?" Cap urged.

"Not her. I found her board. And—Cap, you're gonna want to see this for yourself."

An hour later, we were standing on a rocky beach a few miles south of Alligator Lighthouse. Last night at Chuck's Shuck Shack, we'd tried to be the voices of reason to calm the shark panic, reminding everyone that we still didn't have any evidence that Dr. Edwards had been attacked. She could have just been swept off course by the storm current. We might still find her stranded somewhere. That's what we'd said, anyway.

That hope went out the window when we saw the huge bite mark ripped out of the paddleboard Dougie was guarding.

FRANK

THE ISLAND-WIDE SEARCH HADN'T TURNED UP
EEE, but it had turned up something. The bright
blue-and-green board with wave-patterned trim
stood out on the rocky shoreline like a neon light as
we made our way across the beach toward Dougie.

"That looks like the same board she was on yesterday, all
right," Joe observed.

"With just one big difference," I remarked grimly.

The jagged, half-moon-shaped bite torn from the back of
the board was impossible to miss.

Dougie chewed nervously on his lip, exposing his cracked
incisor as he replayed for Cap what had happened.

"I've been fishing this same stretch of beach every day
for twenty years, so I noticed it right off. Knew from the

color it had to be Trip's, and my heart done leaped thinking I might find her too, but then I took a closer look at her board, and . . ." He trailed off.

Dougie had shown a detective's instincts by leaving the board where he'd found it, partway up the rocky beach where the tide appeared to have carried it. Protocol is for the first person at the site to leave everything untouched so they don't disturb any evidence or contaminate the crime scene before a forensic expert arrives to make their analysis. I don't know if you could technically call a shark attack a crime scene, but the implications for EEE were just as bad.

As for the evidence, it was obvious enough from the large chunk missing from the rear of the board that it had been made by a shark, but that still left a pretty large suspect pool. If Dougie had moved the board, I might never have spotted the smoking gun the perp left behind. Only in this case, the smoking gun wasn't a gun at all. It was a tooth.

The sun peeked through the clouds as I leaned over to examine the board, sending a glint of light off something embedded in the jaw-shaped bite.

"There's a tooth still stuck in the board!" I exclaimed.

Cap and Dougie leaned in as I gently pulled it out. The serration on the blade of the sharply angled tooth was a dead giveaway.

"Tiger shark," Cap and I both said at the same time.

Shark jaws are built like conveyor belts with multiple rows of teeth, and they're constantly growing new ones. When they lose a tooth hunting, a new tooth rotates in from the row behind to replace it. Sharks lose teeth all the time, but to actually find one embedded in a paddleboard was shocking.

Dougie gave a low whistle. "That's a big chomper. Gotta be at least an inch and a half."

Cap's shoulders slumped. "The kind of tooth you'd expect to see on a shark with a dorsal fin the size of the one we saw yesterday."

I could hear the defeat in his voice. It was hard to draw any conclusion except one: Ron, the mayor, Captain Diamond, and the other anti-shark alarmists at the Shuck Shack had been right about what happened to Dr. Edwards. The same shark we'd seen had attacked her.

We couldn't make the argument that EEE had been blown off course in the storm anymore. We could only hope she'd escaped the shark unharmed and taken shelter onshore somewhere after the attack.

A shiver ran down my spine. We'd still been in the water when we'd spotted the shark's dorsal fin. If that storm hadn't forced the rest of us to make for shore early, Joe and I would have been right in the shark's path, beside EEE when it attacked. I could tell from the look on his face that Joe was thinking the same thing.

"It could have been any of us," he whispered.

The search continued for a few more bleak hours before the rain became too heavy and Cap gave *Sally*'s crew the command to head for shore. They were the first words he'd spoken since the morning.

When we got back to the marina, the shark attack wasn't the only thing on people's minds. Everyone was heading to the same place—town hall.

"The town council vote!" I'd been so focused on my search duties aboard the R/V, I'd forgotten all about the big meeting to decide the fate of the resort development.

"Well, we're here. We might as well go check it out," Joe suggested as we fell in with the crowd heading a couple of blocks inland.

"Wow, I bet the whole town is here," I said as we filed into the packed room, grabbing two of the last seats.

"It's standing room only!" Joe said, looking back at people still pushing their way in.

As everyone settled down, one detail jumped out, setting the tone for the whole meeting: the empty seat on the dais where EEE would have been seated among the other council members. A little plaque was set up on the table in front of her seat as a reminder that Councilwoman Edwards wouldn't be coming.

"It sounds like everyone realizes Trip would have been the deciding vote against the development," I said to Joe as I looked at all the concerned faces in the audience and overheard fragments of the heated conversations happening around us.

Joe shifted in his seat. "The vote is about sharks, too,

since it's the lemon shark nursery that's holding things up. I'm no doctor, but I think this town has come down with a bad case of shark fever."

"I'm afraid it's the sharks that are going to get the wrong end of that diagnosis," I whispered as Mayor Boothby strode up to his seat at the center of the table and brought the meeting to order with a bang of his gavel.

"Ladies and gentlemen of Lookout, the vote on the Mangrove Palace Resort development plan on this evening's agenda"—the mayor paused dramatically—"has been postponed."

There was a sudden eruption of reactions from the surprised crowd—sighs of relief from those against the development, groans and angry shouts from the development's supporters, including Ron, Captain Diamond, and a whole bunch of others. Oddly, Maxwell himself wasn't one of them. I turned to see him quietly nodding approval from his seat in the back.

"Huh, you'd think he'd be yelling the loudest," Joe commented. "Without Trip here to stop him, his project sounded like a slam dunk."

"It's like the development's opponents snatched victory from the jaws of defeat," I said without thinking first. Joe and I both cringed. "Sorry. That came out wrong. What I meant was, this could give the development's opponents a chance to rally more support against it."

Cap was sitting a couple of rows in front of us, staring at

the dais with his mouth hanging open. Talk about a lot for one guy to process in a single day. The postponement was an unexpected victory for Shark Lab's cause, but without the lab's director, it was bittersweet. I could understand why he wasn't joining in the cheering.

Mayor Boothby motioned everyone to settle down. "We have bigger fish to fry today, my friends. In light of the horrible tragedy—nay, horrible *assault*—that has befallen our beloved councilwoman Dr. E. Ella Edwards, I have deemed it necessary to postpone all other town matters until our current crisis is addressed. In memory of my dear, departed colleague, I am now calling an emergency meeting to present my new anti-shark defense initiative."

I watched as Cap's mouth dropped open even farther. His wasn't the only one.

"Trip could still be out there! We still might find her!" Chuck called out, earning shouts of approval from others in the room.

"I have just received word that the coast guard has changed the status of their search from a search and rescue to search and recovery," Boothby continued, ignoring the outburst. "Councilwoman Edwards is tragically gone, and we need to make sure she's the last one to suffer this horrible fate." He pounded his fist on the table. "We need to make this town safe again from the cartilaginous man-eaters that are invading our shores!"

The room erupted in a competing chorus of cheers and jeers.

"The mayor's right! It's us or the sharks!" Ron yelled, leaping out of his seat.

"Did you see the news?" a curly-haired councilwoman seated to Boothby's left asked. "The attack on Dr. Edwards was one of the big national stories. It's got the tourists scared. I had three cancellations at the hotel today."

"It's not just the tourists who are scared," an elderly councilman said. "I'm afraid to step into the water in my own town. And my grandkids— I had nightmares last night just thinking about it."

Mayor Boothby nodded along vigorously with each new complaint. "How much more can we let our economy suffer because of this threat? How many more of our loved ones must be lost to this menace?"

"How many more?" Chuck asked incredulously. "There's only been one in the past thirty years! More people are injured in car and boating accidents every day."

"And cows!" Joe shouted, looking at me for approval.

That may not have been exactly how I would have used that statistic, but it did underline just how rare attacks were—a fact that unfortunately seemed to be entirely lost on the mayor, and from the sound of the crowd, at least half the people at the meeting.

Cap had been looking more and more pained since the opening gavel. It was a lot harder to convince people that sharks weren't to blame now that EEE's board had been found. Defending the animal that had attacked his partner might have seemed weird to some people, but EEE had been one of the world's biggest shark advocates, and I knew that was what she would want him to do.

Cap stood up, clearing his throat before addressing the crowd. "When attacks do happen, they're terrible tragedies, of course, but out of hundreds of millions of people in the water around the world each year, there are only a handful of fatalities because of shark attacks. You act like it's us under siege, but it's the other way around." Now that he had everyone's full attention, he seemed more confident as he continued. "I wouldn't have known this if it weren't for Trip, but as many as two hundred million sharks are killed by people every year. More than we can count have their fins cut off and sold for the shark fin soup trade. Millions more are tossed away as bycatch by commercial fishing fleets or overfished by the food industry as a cheap alternative for frozen fish products. Then they're mislabeled or nicknamed something tastier-sounding, so a lot of the time, people don't even realize what they're eating."

Joe groaned. "I'm going to have to start taking a closer look at the ingredients in my fish sticks."

"Tons more are killed for sport, or just out of plain fear, including many species that are totally harmless," Cap continued. "And the sharks that are left have to survive in water clogged with our plastic trash while facing trauma from changes in temperature and acidity thanks to global warming."

A councilman in a bow tie to Boothby's left nodded

somberly. "These are all issues the town council could be helping to change instead of stoking people's fears. That's what Trip would want."

Cap put his hand to his heart. "Dr. Edwards knew better than anyone that the oceans are in trouble, and sharks are some of the biggest victims."

A lot of people nodded along and murmured their agreement. Just as many didn't, though.

"Councilwoman Edwards was the victim yesterday!" the elderly councilman shouted.

"Of course we're afraid!" yelled a man from the crowd.

"I get that people are scared, but what happened to Trip was one-in-a-million bad luck," Cap said sadly. "She'd be the first one to tell you that sharks are worth a lot more to our community alive. And not just because of their environmental value. Protecting them is good for our economy. Ecotourism has become big business. No other creature on earth captures people's imaginations like sharks do, and people spend tons of money traveling all over the world to dive with sharks and even to go on conservation expeditions."

"I see how all the youngsters go to Scuba-Doo and the other dive outfits so they can get the shark selfies to put on their Graham Crackergram and Snapplechats and whatnots," Dougie offered, looking at the back row, where the scraggly scuba instructor we'd seen at Chuck's was chewing intently on his fingernails. "Ain't that right, Shaggy?"

"Disrespecting sharks is bad karma," Shaggy sort-of

answered in a mumble, slipping down in his seat. He didn't seem like the type of guy who liked to have the spotlight on him.

"They're good for folks like me in the local charter business too," Dougie added. "There's no sports fishing without sporty fish."

Cap nodded. "Trip always said that sharks are a renewable financial resource—so long as you protect them. And that's without even going into all the data she had on the long-term global economic impact of declining fishery populations and how maintaining a healthy ocean ecosystem benefits all of us."

"Captain, what benefits us most right now is not getting eaten by sharks!" the mayor shot back.

Joe leaned over. "Wow, this dude is a pro at ignoring facts and redirecting the conversation where he wants."

"He's not even trying to address anyone's concerns except the ones he already agrees with," I replied.

"The only thing I care about is keeping my citizens safe!" Boothby persisted emphatically.

"You don't care about protecting us," Cap thundered back. "You're preying on people's fears to justify doing something irrational and politically self-serving."

Chuck stood up with her hands on her hips. "Mayor, you know I love you like a misguided older brother, but anyone with their eyes open can see you're trying to distract us from all your scandals and trying to get folks to keep voting for you."

"My eyes are closed with the truth!" Ron declared, stabbing the air with his finger.

"What does that even mean, Ron?" Chuck asked, exasperated.

"The only scandal here is what's happening on our beaches," Boothby insisted. "I'm authorizing the release of Lookout Key's emergency fund to build an underwater shark wall—"

There was a collective gasp. Even the people who supported the mayor seemed stunned by the announcement, including his fellow council members.

"And," Boothby continued, "to pay a bounty for every shark caught by a citizen of Lookout Key!"

The murmurs grew even louder. Half the room seemed appalled, and the other half elated. Cap was literally speechless; well, unless you count turning bright red as speech. On the other side of the room, Diamond was pumping his tattooed fist in the air.

"Cha-ching!" he shouted.

"The town is suddenly flush with money for this, but you couldn't afford to fix up a historical landmark like Alligator Lighthouse?" Chuck demanded.

"And we still need new textbooks for the high school. Where's the money for that?" the councilman in the bow tie snapped.

"You can't just release funds without consulting us! That kind of expenditure will blow up the budget!" a second council member protested.

"Lives are at stake, ladies and gentlemen," Mayor Boothby insisted. "We need to take action, and we need to take it now!"

Cap's face had, if possible, gone even redder. I started to feel myself turning red as well. Joe and I had come to Lookout Key to study and help protect sharks. As shaken as I still was by the shark-chomped paddleboard I'd seen that morning, an indiscriminate cull of every shark in the area didn't make any sense. If Joe and I approached detecting that way, well . . .

"Trying to get rid of every shark because of one isolated attack would be like arresting every single person with freckles just because one freckled person committed a crime," I called, standing up so I could be heard. "It would be unjust!"

"Killing sharks willy-nilly isn't even legal," the councilman with the bow tie said. "Every self-respecting fisherperson knows there are limits on how many sharks you can catch, and which kinds."

"It ain't just what's good for the fish, either," Dougie chimed in. "Like Cap said, it's good for business, too. I bet half the people in this room rely on sea life to make a living one way or another. What tourist is gonna pay to come here to catch or take a picture of a thing that don't exist no more?"

There were rumbles of approval. Maybe the town hall tide was turning. "Removing catch restrictions isn't the only thing that's illegal," I added. "Unscientific gimmicks like underwater nets and barriers like the one you're proposing aren't just against the law in a lot of places—there's no proof they work. Mostly they just waste money, disrupt delicate ecosystems, and kill innocent sea life. And not just sharks. Sea turtles and dolphins, too."

"That's a sacrifice I'm willing to make," Boothby replied. "I'm evoking my mayoral authority to keep the citizens of Lookout Key safe. My anti-shark initiative goes into effect immediately."

"You're not even going to vote on this?" Chuck asked in disbelief.

"We don't need a vote. I'm the mayor!"

The curly-haired councilwoman seated to Boothby's left tugged on his sleeve. "Um, actually, Mayor, we kind of do. It's in the town bylaws."

"It's decided, then!" Boothby concluded. If he felt the councilwoman yanking on his arm, he didn't show any sign of it. "My anti-shark initiative begins tomorrow. Happy hunting!" With that, Mayor Boothby banged his gavel on the table and marched victoriously off the dais.

Joe and I turned to face each other, dismayed.

"I think this case just turned from one mission into two," Joe said. "To try to find Trip—"

I finished the thought for him. "And protect the sharks that are accused of eating her."

NO GUTS, NO GLORY

6

JOE

"I DON'T KNOW IF WE JUST WITNESSED A TOWN council meeting or a circus!" I told Frank as we stood outside town hall, watching the crowd leave.

"All I know is Ringleader Boothby just made our case a lot harder."

My bro and I had worked a lot of big cases, and this wasn't the first time we'd seen normal people do some pretty goofy things during a crisis. Sometimes when people are scared, they make head-scratching decisions because they want to feel like something's being done, even when what they do winds up hurting them or their town in the long run—like trying to get rid of all of Lookout's sharks. That didn't make all the anti-shark supporters bad guys. It's hard to be patient and listen to reason when you're afraid. It just stinks when unscrupulous bigwigs like Mayor Boothby take advantage of the fear instead of trying to find solutions that actually help.

"Guys like Boothby can be a lot more dangerous than any shark, if you ask me," I said.

"Speaking of big fish"—Frank pointed to Maxwell shaking hands and hobnobbing as he strolled out of the town hall toward us—"seems strange that one was so quiet. You'd think he'd be more worked up about the development vote getting postponed."

"Why don't we ask him about it?" I suggested, stepping up to cut him off before he could pass by.

"Hi, Mr. Maxwell!" I said, extending my hand. "Got a minute to chat?"

He didn't hesitate to take my hand, but the handshake was accompanied by a confused look. It only lasted for a second, though, before his features shifted into a cheery smile. "Ah, yes. The young detectives from up north! I'd been hoping to make your acquaintance. How are you enjoying your stay in the Conch Republic?"

"You know who we are?" Frank asked, eyeing Maxwell suspiciously.

"Oh, indeed. This is a small island, and it's good business to know what's going on. You're not the only ones with an eye on things." He tapped the side of his perfectly styled head.

"Speaking of things that are good for business, that meeting could have gone a lot better for you if the vote went ahead as planned," I said.

Maxwell gave an unconcerned shrug. "You win some, you lose some. And sometimes, you can win one and still lose. I want the support of the community. If we'd won that vote without Dr. Edwards there on the same day we found out she was attacked, I'd permanently lose the respect of half the people on Lookout Key. I live here too, and Mangrove Palace isn't the only project I have in the works. It doesn't do me any good to come off looking like an opportunistic vulture."

"So the delay is more good business," Frank said pointedly.

If Maxwell was thrown by Frank's accusatory tone, he didn't show it. This guy was smooth sailing all the way.

"It was the right thing to do, *and* it's good business. Like your friend Cap suggested when he argued against the mayor's ludicrous shark proposal: doing well and doing good don't have to be mutually exclusive. Flaunting my victory during a tragedy would be a rotten way to show my love for the community. And I'm not just talking about public appearances. I like to be able to look myself in the mirror as much as the next guy. The notion may be foreign to our dear mayor, but a thing can be both proper and profitable."

My eyebrows went up. "I'd think you'd be on board the mayor's anti-shark boat, seeing as it's sharks swimming in the way of your resort."

"That boat is not a particularly seaworthy ship, if you catch my drift." Maxwell grinned. "I find Boothby useful at times, but following his lead can leave a stink on you if you're not careful. The mayor likes to fall back on stunt shows and scare tactics like that shark wall nonsense because he doesn't have anything of substance to offer voters once they look past the smoke screen. I prefer to win people over with reason."

Mr. Reason was sounding a lot more reasonable than I'd expected, and I couldn't help wondering what his whole "I've got nothing to hide" act might be covering up.

"Besides, it's not the sharks' fault," he continued with a laugh. "I don't have anything against sharks or Dr. Edwards, for that matter. Our priorities may not be the same, but I do respect her and the work she does, even if we don't see eye to eye on the subject of my latest project."

Frank and I couldn't help exchanging a look. Was this guy saying all the right things because he actually meant them, or was this all a show to win us over?

"It's true," he insisted. "In fact, I've donated a healthy sum of money to Shark Lab over the years. I made another contribution just this morning to help fund Captain Rogers's search-and-rescue effort. I know the R/V isn't cheap to run. It would be a shame to have to divert the lab's resources away from its research." He smiled. "*Even* if some of it may be used to hold up my development."

Maxwell clapped us both on the shoulder. "I truly do hope you boys are successful in your investigation to find Dr. Edwards. If I can be of any further assistance, please don't hesitate to ask."

"Go figure." I turned back to Frank as Maxwell sauntered

away. "I wasn't expecting him to be a supporter of our Anti-Anti-Shark Counter-Initiative."

"The whole town has their boat rocked over this thing, and he's leisure cruising right through the center of the storm." Frank sounded impressed. "No wonder that guy's so successful. He's a pro at laying on the charm."

"Including on us?" I asked, wondering how much we could actually trust what Maxwell had just told us. "I'm still on Team Lemon Shark when it comes to his development plans messing with the baby shark nursery, but I can't help it. I kinda like the dude."

We started our third day on Lookout standing on the marina dock, watching the sun rise while we waited for Cap to show up for the day's search.

"Two hours late. I hope he's okay," Frank said, looking at his watch.

Cap stumbled toward us a few minutes later, looking bleary-eyed.

"You can blame the mayor," he said before we could ask him what had happened. "I was getting threatening calls all night from one of his anti-shark supporters. I barely slept."

"Do you know who it was?" I asked, shifting instantly into investigation mode.

Cap shook his head. "Whoever it was just kept playing the theme song from *Jaws* over and over."

"Could it have been Diamond?" Frank asked.

"Tormenting you with a movie about hunting man-eating sharks seems about his style."

Cap growled, walking past us toward the small motorboat we'd be taking out to where the R/V was anchored. "Don't even say his name. Besides, he wouldn't have wasted the sleep. He's probably already been on the water for hours trying to collect on the mayor's bounty."

He yawned, then let out a disgusted grunt. "We've got a lot of time to make up. I'm going to have the crew pulling double duty looking for Trip and patrolling for shark poachers. As soon as the council meeting let out, I was on the phone with the Fish and Wildlife Conservation Commission to tell them about the mayor's illegal shark hunt. They'll have extra boats out to crack down on anyone we catch."

We were still a few feet from the boat when it hit me. . . .

I gagged. "What is that smell?"

"Is that coming from our boat?" Frank asked, pulling his T-shirt over his face.

Cap ran ahead and then stopped suddenly. We ran up to join him, and my eyes went wide as I took in the scene.

The inside of the motorboat was filled with rotting chum!

The smell wasn't the worst part, though. In the middle of all the bloody fish guts, someone had scrawled:

SHARK BAIT, GO HOME

RARE FISH 7

FRANK

IT WAS A SHORT BUT VERY STINKY BOAT RIDE OUT to the R/V.

As soon as we got on board, Kat alerted Cap that they were tracking a number of suspicious fishing boats on the *Sally*'s radar. It didn't take a detective to figure out that most of them were out hunting sharks, hoping to cash in on the mayor's bounty—or that Cap and his crew wouldn't be very popular trying to stand in their way. It seemed likely that one or more of the mercenaries were responsible for the prank calls and fish guts, just probably not Diamond. Cap had been right about his rival being laser-focused on fishing—radio chatter from the other boats confirmed that the shark hunter had been the first one spotted heading out that morning.

As the newest "members" of the *Sally*'s crew, Joe and I were given the not-so-awesome job of washing the chum out of the motorboat, which had been lifted onto the deck by one of the R/V's cranes.

"Time to earn your keep, greenhorns." Kat smiled slyly on her way below deck. "Greenhorn" was the not-entirely-affectionate term for a crew's newbie.

"Give them a break, Kat," Cap called after her as we got to work with our buckets and sponges. "There's no such thing as an unimportant job on a vessel like this. Besides, having the greenhorns clean up fish guts is a time-honored tradition."

"Oh, I feel honored all right," Joe grumbled, giving the stink eye to the red goop dripping off his sponge.

Cap grinned. It was the first smile I'd seen on his face in a while.

Since it seemed like he was in a decent mood, I figured this might be a good chance to multitask and gather more intel on the local anti-shark population while we cleaned. "It seems pretty generous of Maxwell to donate money to the search effort, even when Trip stands in the way of his development."

The initial surprise on Cap's face melted away. "Figures he's already gotten around to smooth-talking you. Boothby may hold the official title, but the real mayor of this town is that eel. Never misses an opportunity to campaign for his real estate deals. He's tried to butter up every member of my crew at some point, thinking he can infiltrate the ranks and change our minds."

"He's pretty buttery," Joe confirmed, looking up from the patch of gunk he'd been scrubbing.

"Maxwell made it sound like he's been a big donor for a while," I said.

"Research isn't cheap, and Maxwell's development projects never posed a problem in the past. We got our last check in the mail the same day he announced plans for Mangrove Palace. It was way more than he'd ever given us, and would have paid for a lot of research," Cap said wistfully. "We realized why once we read the plan's fine print. That kind of payoff may work for the mayor, but not Shark Lab. Trip sent it back that day with a note suggesting he invest his money in finding a new resort location, because she was going to make sure this one never got approved."

"Maxwell conveniently forgot to mention that part when we talked to him," I said, shaking a piece of fish goop off my arm.

"Are you going to send back the donation he gave you yesterday too?" Joe asked.

Cap looked uncomfortable. "Didn't have a choice this time. Sometimes as a captain you have to make hard calls. This is about finding Trip, and that money helps us do it. We got a few other small donations, but not enough to make a real difference. We may do big things at Shark Lab, but we're still a small operation. The overhead's high and the lab doesn't have a lot of money socked away for contingencies. I need to make sure we're out on the water searching. Trip can't conduct any of the great research we're trying to do if she's not with us."

Joe and I both nodded somberly.

"Trip is the heart and soul of Shark Lab. Without her—" Cap frowned. "I don't know what we're going to do if we don't find her. The lab's research budget covers all our operation and fuel costs. I feel like a total selfish jerk worrying about myself at a time like this, but I can't swing both the R/V bank payments and fuel on my own, let alone pay the crew. They rely on *Sally* as much as I do. If I lost her . . ." He trailed off. "The crew on a vessel like this is a kind of family. I'm the captain. I can't let everyone down. I have to get Trip back on board."

Cap's determination to find Dr. Edwards was really moving. I didn't have the heart to tell him it was out of his control—and the odds weren't looking good.

"We're going to do everything we can to help," I said as confidently as I could. I'm not sure how convincing it sounded coming from a chum-covered greenhorn.

I saw a familiar gleam in my brother's eyes. Knowing Joe, this could go one of two ways, and I sure hoped it was the really smart, practical detective path and not the ridiculously risky "what did we get ourselves into" one.

"I think I have a better way for us to help than this," he said, squeezing the fish guts out of his sponge.

"Getting your hands dirty and doing the unpleasant jobs is an important part of crew work," Cap scolded. "I didn't get to be a captain without scrubbing my share of guts."

"I agree, Captain, but now that the guts are almost scrubbed, maybe Frank and I can put this motorboat to better use. There's only so much we can do to help with the search on board the R/V. Not that chum-scrubbing duty isn't important, but the place where my bro and I really do our best work is in the field. We could cover more ground if you let us use the motorboat to search the shallow water closer to shore where Trip might have washed up."

Cap took a moment to consider Joe's proposal. "Can't do it. You need a boating license to legally operate it."

Joe grinned. "Well, it's a good thing I took that boating course and registered for my license before coming down here. I'm one hundred percent aboveboard!"

"Still can't do it, Joe," Cap insisted. "Shark Lab is responsible for your safety while you're here, and our insurance only covers actual crew members. I can't afford to take any more financial risks right now."

This time, I was the one who grinned. "If I read the fine print right, we're covered by Bayport Aquarium's insurance policy while we're here, not the lab's, so you're not on the hook if anything goes wrong."

"Which it won't!" Joe assured him.

Cap stared out toward the shoreline a few hundred yards away. "Clear weather and calm seas. It *would* expand the search, and I can't spare any of my crew." He sighed. "Permission granted. You have exactly two hours."

A few minutes later, Joe and I were in the water headed toward shore.

"I knew getting that boating license would come in handy," Joe said from behind the wheel. "Make way for Captain Joe! Master of the high seas!"

"You know, Joe—" I began.

"*Captain* Joe."

I laughed. "I'm not calling you 'captain.'"

"Admiral?" he asked.

My smile faded as my original thought came back to me. "Do you think there was anything strange about the wording of that threatening message this morning?"

"You mean, besides it being written in rotting fish guts?" Joe asked.

"Maybe I'm overthinking it, but why would the person specifically write 'Go Home' instead of, like, 'Back Off'? If you think about it, Lookout Key *is* the home of Cap and the rest of his crew. We're the only ones whose home is over a thousand miles away."

"Oh . . . ," Joe said slowly as my meaning sank in. "You think that threat was meant for *us*?"

"Maxwell knows we're helping Cap's search and that we're detectives, so plenty of other locals could too."

"Ron and some of the other anti-shark gang heard Chuck hire us the other night," Joe reminded me. "If any of them are caught up in something shady and know we're detecting, they could be afraid of what we might turn up in the process."

"Even if what we turned up was Trip Edwards alive and well, that could throw a major wrench in both Maxwell's and Boothby's works. And there are a lot of other people who benefit from both the development and the anti-shark initiative. Anyone who knows Cap must know he's too strong-willed to let a message like that stop him. They don't know us, though, and they might think a couple teenagers from out of town *would* be scared by a warning smeared in fish blood."

"You're right. They don't know us. If they did, they'd know threats like that only make the Hardy boys more determined." Joe's smile slipped. "And, um, maybe just a little bit scared. I mean, who wants to be turned into shark bait? But mostly, determined."

"Like you said before, Chuck hired us to detect, so let's get to it." I pointed at the shoreline. "Full speed ahead, Captain!"

We spent the next hour cruising slowly through the little channels carved into the coastline a few miles south of the marina. There weren't any beaches here. Just a lot of lush green foliage and mangrove trees, with their tangled roots actually growing out of salt water. Joe cut the engine and let the current carry us into a channel that looked like a promising place for someone to seek shelter during a storm.

I had my eyes glued to my binoculars when a shock of unkempt, dirty blond hair popped out from behind a tree and into my field of vision. I adjusted the focus, and the head the hair belonged to came into view.

"Shaggy!" I whispered.

"Huh?" Joe whispered back, pointing his binoculars in the same direction as mine. "Shaggy? What's he doing out here? This doesn't look like much of a scuba-diving spot."

"And he doesn't have any gear with him. Just a knapsack."

The gangly owner of the Scuba-Doo Dive School looked furtively around, like he was afraid someone might be watching. Luckily, he only glanced our way for a second before continuing toward the water. The trees between us must have been good camouflage.

We were only about twenty yards away when he unzipped his knapsack and pulled out a bundle wrapped in a Scuba-Doo Dive School sweatshirt. He gave another nervous look around before unwrapping it.

"What in the world . . . ?" I whispered as we watched Shaggy pull out what looked like a large fin.

Joe gasped. "Is that a shark fin?"

"Do you think Shaggy is involved in the illegal shark fin trade?" I hissed.

"Like what Cap said at the town hall meeting about people cutting off fins to put in soup?" Joe asked.

I could feel my hands balling into fists. "Finning is the worst. Some people think shark fin soup has medicinal benefits, but that's bogus. It's really just cartilage. That doesn't stop it from being a huge luxury dish in China and other countries, though. The market's massive. We're talking tens of millions of sharks finned every year, worldwide. It's one of the biggest reasons why populations have declined so much."

Joe growled, "Don't people realize what they're doing to the ocean?"

"Oh, it gets worse. Most of the time, the finners don't even use the whole shark; they just throw the bodies back in the water to sink while the shark's still alive! Thankfully, more people are learning about how awful it is, and a lot of countries are finally cracking down on the practice." I stared through my binoculars at the fin in Shaggy's hands. "There's a lot more cracking down to do, though."

"Chuck seemed surprised the other night when Shaggy was able to pay cash for his meal. If he's selling shark fins, that might explain why he suddenly has dough," Joe theorized.

I adjusted the focus on my binoculars, trying to get a better look. "Is he tying rocks to the fin?"

"It looks like it, but if he went to the trouble of getting the fin, why would he throw it away?"

"Unless he's afraid of getting caught with it. Cap said the Fish and Wildlife Commission was on high alert for illegal shark fishing."

Joe nodded from behind his binoculars. "Maybe he's

worried the mayor's shark hunt is going to bring heat down on him."

"Yeah, but unfortunately, it's not actually illegal to sell fins in the US if they're removed from the shark once it's on shore," I said, sharing some more of the research I'd done ahead of our trip. "It's only cutting them off while the shark is still on the boat that's illegal. It's a loophole a lot of smugglers use to get around the law, since it's so hard to tell a legal fin from an illegal one. A lot of states have banned shark fins altogether, but Florida's behind the curve. It's been one of the biggest importers of shark fins in the entire country!" I could feel my temper rising and made sure to lower my voice so I didn't give away our position. "Shaggy could sell the fin if he wanted to and it still wouldn't be illegal."

"So why's he getting rid of it?" Joe insisted.

"Let's ask him," I said through gritted teeth.

Joe hit the boat's engine and gunned it toward Shaggy. Birds squawked and took flight as the sound of the motor broke the silence. So did our perp. He turned to flee as soon as he saw us coming, only he tripped over a mangrove root and splashed face-first into the water without making it five feet.

I leaped out of the boat as soon we hit shallow enough water, and was standing over him before he could get back on his feet. Joe dropped anchor and was standing on his other side a moment later.

"That fin doesn't belong to you," I said.

"It's not mine!" Shaggy shouted, holding the fin out in front of him like a gruesome shield.

"You don't say? And here I thought all scuba instructors came equipped with their own dorsal fins," Joe quipped.

"I never wanted it!" Shaggy cried. "I didn't know it would call another shark. I didn't mean for anything bad to happen, I swear. I—I think it's cursed."

Joe gave me a baffled look. "Do you have any idea what he's talking about?"

"You can have it! I don't want! I—I was just going to give it back to the sharks," Shaggy babbled on. "As a—an offering so they don't come for me next."

"An offering?" I repeated, trying to make sense of his rambling. "To the sharks?"

"Just—just get it away from me, please!" He held the fin out as far as his arms would reach.

The idea of touching a severed shark fin made my stomach turn, but confiscating it to take back to the R/V for Shark Lab to document was the responsible thing to do. I took a deep breath and grabbed the fin.

The fin was a lot harder than I'd expected. Almost like . . .

"Is that plastic?" I stared at the object in my hands in disbelief.

Joe quickly took it from me, tapped it with his knuckles, and then flipped it over. "Other than the strip of Velcro on the bottom, I'd say yeah. And—" He squinted closer to read the tiny words printed next to it. "'Made in America.' Unless there's a super-rare species of plastic shark I've never heard of, I don't think we have to worry about Shaggy being tied up in the fin trade. This fin's a phony."

"Why are you in such a hurry to get rid of a toy fin?" I asked.

"Well, um, did you hear about the other day when everyone spotted that shark swimming near the beach right before Dr. Edwards got attacked?" asked Shaggy.

Joe looked skeptical. "You must not get out of the Mystery Machine much. Everyone on Lookout knows about that. Half of America does. It's been all over the news."

"Oh . . . ," Shaggy whimpered. "Um, I was kinda the shark."

DON'T FAKE THE FUNK

8

JOE

THE PIECES SNAPPED INTO PLACE AS SOON as Shaggy said he was the shark we'd seen—kind of like how that fake fin must have snapped onto Shaggy's back.

"The dorsal fin we saw was a fake, and you were the one doing the faking? No wonder you're trying to get rid of it."

"It wasn't my fault!" he whined.

Frank scratched his head. "Let me get this straight. You snuck into the water with your scuba gear on without anyone knowing and went for a swim with a fake shark fin strapped to your back on a public beach where it was sure to cause mass panic, and it *wasn't* your fault?"

First he nodded yes. Then he shook his head no. Even his nodding was perplexing.

"I didn't want to do it. And I'm not the one who ate Dr. Edwards! I wouldn't ever."

"Well, it's good to know you wouldn't eat a person, Shaggy," I assured him. "I was really worried there for a second. Now what in the world are you talking about?"

"When I got the package, I just thought it was a harmless prank, but then a real shark ate Dr. Edwards, and I'm the one who summoned it!" he wailed. "I swear I didn't know she was missing until after I got to Chuck's later that night. After I wore the fin, I just swam away and went home like the note told me. At first I thought maybe it was just a coincidence, you know, her going missing right after, but then her board washed up all bitten into like that. That's how I knew I summoned a real shark to eat her!"

Shaggy buried his face in his hands and moaned. He still wasn't exactly making sense, but at least more pieces were starting to fall into place.

"So someone sent you a package with the fin and a note asking you to wear it?" Frank pressed.

"Of course not! If they'd asked me, I'd have said no. I mean, I didn't think anyone would get hurt, but pranking people is still kind of mean. And I wouldn't have done it just for the money, either. Not that I can't use it. But once I found out I'd caused a real shark to eat her, I donated all five hundred dollars to her lab. Well, four hundred seventy-three dollars of it, at least. I bought some shrimp. And some lottery tickets."

The contents of the package Shaggy said he'd received were becoming clearer—fake fin, note, money—which also accounted for the cash-for-shrimp transaction that had surprised Chuck, as well as one of the smaller donations Cap said Shark Lab received along with Maxwell's. An important chunk of the story was still missing, though.

"So if you thought the prank was mean and you didn't do it for the money, then why do it at all?"

"Oh, no reason really," he said, laughing nervously.

It looked like Shaggy's willing cooperation was over. I was going to have to take drastic measures.

"I guess I'll just have to give this cursed plastic fin back to you, then," I said, holding the phony dorsal fin out to him.

Shaggy recoiled. And then he started talking.

"They threatened to tell my girlfriend about all the money I lost at Chuck's poker games," he blabbed, staring guiltily at his hands. "Which, um, maybe I promised my girlfriend I wouldn't go to anymore because she said she'd leave me if I didn't stop playing, but, well, I found my lucky rabbit's foot, and it seemed like a good omen, and it would be bad luck not to listen to an *omen*, right? But I guess I was wrong, because I lost everything in the Scuba-Doo register, and, um, the safe, too."

"Blackmail," Frank concluded as Shaggy finished his

rambling gambling confession. "I'm guessing the blackmailer wasn't kind enough to sign their name, were they?"

"Uh-huh," Shaggy said matter-of-factly.

"They did?" Frank and I blurted at the same time. Was the solution really going to be this easy?

"It was signed Bruce Quint, but I don't know anybody on Lookout by that name. Or anybody anywhere, really."

"I do," I said, letting out a disappointed sigh. So much for it being easy.

"You know him?" Shaggy asked in surprise.

"Not personally, and I don't think we'll be interrogating him next," I said. "I do happen to be a fan of classic horror flicks, though. Quint was the name of the old guy in *Jaws*, and Bruce was the nickname the filmmakers gave to the mechanical great white shark that eats everybody in the movie."

"Whoa, that's a weird coincidence that the guy who left the note has the same name as the shark in the movie," Shaggy replied, awed.

"It's not his real name, Shaggy. It's meant as a joke," Frank said.

"I don't find it very funny," he muttered.

I looked from the fin back to Shaggy. "So who else knows about you losing all that money?"

"Uh, let's see—" Shaggy appeared to be counting in his head. "Everybody, pretty much."

"Everybody?" I asked. "If everybody knows, wouldn't that already include your girlfriend?"

"Not *everybody*. Just everybody in Chuck's Poker Club, which is, well, mostly everybody. It's a big club."

Chuck had made a comment to Ron about him winning a big hand off her, so it wasn't surprising to hear there was a game in town or that she was the one who hosted it. Chuck's Shuck Shack did seem to be the center of Lookout's social universe.

"If so many people already knew, weren't you worried someone would tell your girlfriend anyway, even if you weren't blackmailed?" I asked.

"Nah. That's the first rule of Chuck's Poker Club. You don't talk about Chuck's Poker Club." Shaggy suddenly looked stricken and smacked himself in the face. "I just broke the rule!"

"I think you have bigger problems right now, Shaggy," Frank reminded him.

"But I took the Chuck's Poker Club oath, and it's a bad omen to break an oath! First I summon a shark to eat Dr. Edwards, and now this! I think I'm cursed!"

"You're a pretty superstitious guy, huh, Shaggy?" I asked.

"Well, yeah," he said, looking up at me like I'd asked him a really silly question. "It's bad luck not to be."

"You know, there are ancient cultures where people believed in shark gods who would eat them if they were displeased," Frank commented.

Shaggy's eyes went wide.

"Pretty sure that's not what happened here, Shag," I said. "I don't think the shark attack had anything to do with shark gods or omens, and I definitely don't think you summoned anything."

"You mean, like, maybe it was just a scientific thing? Like my fin attracted them, or I accidentally used shark sign language to tell that other shark to eat Dr. Edwards, or something? It's still my fault!" Shaggy wailed.

"That other shark . . . ," Frank repeated to himself, then trailed off, lost in thought.

"I'm not an expert on shark behavior, but shark sign language seems pretty far-fetched to me," I said.

"So, like, it was just a coincidence that another shark ate her?" he asked.

"Not a coincidence, and you didn't cause it either." Frank grinned confidently and ruffled Shaggy's shag.

Shaggy squinted up at Frank through the hair in his eyes. "Um, what does that leave?"

I was wondering the same thing.

"There is a way Shaggy may have contributed to Trip's disappearance, just not how he thinks," said Frank. "Until now, our only suspect was the shark we saw a few minutes before we heard her scream. But that wasn't a shark at all; someone just wanted us to think it was. If the sighting of the shark everyone thought attacked her was fake—"

I snapped my fingers. "Then the attack itself might be too!"

"Huh?" Shaggy said, clearly not following.

"Everybody assumed the shark swimming by the beach

was the same one that attacked Trip, but it couldn't have been, because that was really you!" I explained. "That leaves only two options. Shark attacks are rare enough to begin with, right? So either the timing of the prank was a super-unlucky coincidence and a real shark randomly attacked Trip while you were swimming around nearby with a fin on your back—or the entire attack was a hoax!"

"Whoever blackmailed you into wearing that fin just wanted us to *think* we'd seen a shark. So maybe they wanted us to think there'd been an attack as well," Frank concluded.

My hopes soared with the possibility that Dr. Edwards was still okay. "Trip is still missing, right? Without her, we don't have any proof that she was actually attacked!"

This time it was Shaggy who was a step ahead of *us*. "Well, I sure didn't bite her paddleboard. Isn't that proof?"

My shoulders slumped. In our excitement to believe Frank's theory that EEE may not have been attacked by a shark after all, we hadn't factored in a key piece of evidence. We'd seen with our own eyes the damage the shark's jaws had inflicted on the paddleboard. So had Cap and Dr. Edwards's research assistant back at the lab, who'd taken the board to analyze as part of an international shark attack study. The truth was gruesome, and there was no way around it: there had been an attack, the bite mark on that paddleboard was real, and the massive tiger shark responsible for it hadn't been made of plastic.

9

ONCE BITTEN

FRANK

MY HEAD WAS SPINNING TRYING TO make sense of the evidence we'd collected. The shark we'd thought we'd seen couldn't have been the one that attacked Trip like everyone thought, because it wasn't a shark at all! But Shaggy was right. Even if the fin we'd seen from shore was a fake, the paddleboard that washed up on that beach yesterday proved beyond a doubt there had been a very real shark attack. Were the two events connected as I'd suspected? Or was Shaggy's phony shark fin really a red herring?

A burst of static from the motorboat's radio stopped me from breaking the situation down further.

"Hardy boys, come in now!" Cap shouted over the radio.

"Where are you? The rendezvous at the R/V was ten minutes ago. Are you okay?"

I radioed back with a brief message that we were fine and were heading to the R/V now. Then we took the fake fin, left a grateful Shaggy behind—we still had unanswered questions, so we made him give us his cell phone number first by threatening to return the fin to him if he refused—and raced back to the R/V in the motorboat.

Cap was pacing the deck, muttering to himself as we boarded. The muttering turned to shouting as soon as he saw us.

"What in the world were you thinking? I gave you an order to be back here in exactly two hours. You think this is some kind of game? People can get hurt out here. I—" He slammed his fist down on the rail, then closed his eyes and took a deep breath.

Getting yelled at during an investigation wasn't new for us. If there was a case to work, that usually meant something bad had happened, and emotions tended to run high. Sometimes, though, when people yell at you, it's not really so much about the thing they say they're mad about, but other things they're feeling.

Cap lowered his voice, then continued calmly. "I'm responsible for the safety of everyone on this vessel. I've already lost one person this week. If anything happens to you boys on my watch—" He took another deep breath. "With everything that's already happened in the last few days, when you boys didn't show up, I started to think the worst."

Aww, I thought, trying to hide my smile from the angry skipper, *Cap cares about us.*

He forgot all about us missing the rendezvous once we told him *why* we'd missed it. Cap stared at us dumbfounded as we recounted Shaggy's story and showed him the fake fin. He turned it over in his hands like it was an alien artifact from outer space.

"Why would anyone do something like that?"

"That's what we want to find out," Joe said. "I think we should keep it on the DL for now. If word gets around town, it could tip the blackmailer off that we're onto their scheme."

"Whatever you boys think is best," Cap agreed. "I know boats and sharks; this whole crime thing is out of my wheelhouse."

"I was hoping we could also take another look at Trip's paddleboard to see if there's anything we missed that might give us a clue about the attack," I said, earning a confused look from Cap.

"What good will that do? The lab techs onshore are already planning to analyze the bite to estimate the shark's size and see if they can figure anything out about its behavior from the angle of approach. As rare as attacks are, they do happen, and the more we can learn about them, the better we'll be able to prevent more tragedies. Trip always said attacks like this are probably cases of mistaken identity—the shark confuses the board's silhouette for a prey animal, like a seal. Tiger sharks are ambush predators, so a strike from the rear wouldn't be unusual. That's what we see when we study them with bait on the R/V. But even if the lab does find out something useful, I don't see how any of it would be connected to this fake fin business."

"Neither do we," Joe admitted. "The type of clue we're looking for falls into the 'we'll know it when we see it' category."

Cap shrugged. "If you think it will help, I guess, sure. I'll put in a call to the lab to have one of the techs stay so you can head over when we get back to shore."

We waited on deck while Cap headed inside to make the call. He returned looking as stunned as he had been when we'd told him about Shaggy.

"The board's gone," he told us.

"What!" Joe and I cried.

"Somebody smashed the back lock and took it from the storage room, along with a bunch of research equipment. The cops are there now. I told them about the chum prank, and they think whatever shark-hating punks vandalized the motorboat did this, too."

"Did the culprit leave another threatening message?" I asked. I had to resist the urge to shiver when I thought about my hunch that this morning's warning was really meant for us.

"No. Whoever it was just dumped chum all over a bunch of expensive gear instead." Cap punched his fist into his palm. "I blame Boothby for riling everybody up with his blasted shark-hunting stunt. I'd better tell the crew to keep their heads up onshore in case these thugs try anything with them."

Was the theft another unlikely coincidence? I wondered

as Cap retreated to break the news to his crew. Or did someone want to make sure no one else examined EEE's board?

"Why do I get the feeling this robbery was about more than troublemaking shark-hating vandals?" Joe asked, echoing my thoughts.

"There's no shortage of shark-hating suspects, either way," I said. "Captain Diamond for one. But Cap's theory that Diamond's been too busy shark hunting to mess around with prank calls or chumming the motorboat makes sense."

"Don't forget Ron," Joe said. "He's one of the mayor's biggest anti-shark cheerleaders, and Cap did threaten to batter him like fried squid at Chuck's the other day."

"It seemed like half the people at the town council meeting were on Team No Shark right along with him," I said. "We don't even know if it really was one of the anti-sharkers. There could be another motive we haven't figured out yet."

"You mean *motives*!" Joe moaned. "This investigation has gone from a missing persons case to a shark attack search-and-rescue to a shark defense mission to a vandalism and harassment case to a shark hoax hunt to grand theft. And we still don't know how or if any of it is connected!"

"Well, let's start by working the one solid lead we actually have," I said, pulling out my phone to call the newest number in my contacts.

Unfortunately, our one lead wasn't answering, and when we made it back to the marina, the Scuba-Doo Dive School shop was locked up tight. According to the woman at the bait shop next door, Shaggy had never made it in to open, which wasn't exactly surprising, given where we'd last seen him.

"I'd hoped a follow-up interview with Shaggy might shake some more suspects loose." I sighed.

But when I looked at Joe, he was grinning. "You said we only have one lead, but I just thought of another one. Who's the one person Shaggy mentioned who definitely knew about him losing all that money in those poker games?"

"The game's hostess!" I shouted. "Feeling hungry, Joe? Because I think a trip to Chuck's Shuck Shack is in order."

Joe rubbed his stomach. "Always. But I doubt she'll break the first rule of the poker club with a bunch of customers around. The Shuck Shack sign said they close at ten on weeknights. I say we slip in at nine forty-five to take Chuck up on those free shrimp, so we're already inside when she locks the doors."

We sat at the bar chowing down on endless shrimp poppers as planned. To make sure we'd still be there after everyone else was gone, Joe ordered three baskets. For each of us. And whale fries with old salt. And calamari. *And* spiny lobster roll sliders. The only thing he passed on was the pickled red herring tacos.

"This case may have too many red herrings already," he'd said. "I don't need them on my tacos, too!"

I'd thought his ordering frenzy was going a little

overboard, but it turned out he was just really hungry. He was still stuffing his face at closing time!

Chuck had already asked us for an update on the search for EEE when she served us our food. Word had spread about the chum stink bomb and the stolen board, but we conveniently forgot to mention our run-in with Shaggy and his fake fin. At ten fifteen, Chuck started clearing her throat and yawning conspicuously in our direction.

"Okay, boys. I know I offered you all the free shrimp you can eat, and I don't want to rush you, but I'd really like to get home," she finally told us at 10:32, when the last of her staff had left for the night and the three of us were the only ones there. "Can I get a doggie bag for you guys to take the rest of that to go? I promise you can come back tomorrow morning for all the pink shrimp breakfast burritos you can cram down your gullets."

"I'll see your breakfast burritos and raise you everything you can tell us about the guest list at Chuck's Poker Club," Joe replied, popping another shrimp into his mouth for emphasis.

Chuck crossed her arms and stared us down for a minute before replying. "Somebody broke the first rule of the poker club." She grabbed a shrimp out of Joe's hand and tossed it into her own mouth. "I can't let you join, if that's what you're getting at. Pretty sure letting minors play in a high-stakes poker game is against bigger rules than mine."

"Oh, I'm pretty sure underground high-stakes poker

games are against the rules for adults, too, but we're not interested in busting you, and we don't want to play," I told her. "We're here to get to the bottom of all the other rules that have been broken in the last few days."

"If you're talking about this whole anti-shark mess the mayor started and whoever's messing with Shark Lab, then I'm with you, but I don't see what that has to do with my little bitty game."

"Your little bitty game is causing big problems. One of your members is using Shaggy's losses to blackmail him, and we need to figure out who," Joe said.

Chuck recoiled like she was genuinely surprised, but that didn't mean she wasn't bluffing. I had expected the hostess of a secret poker club to have a good poker face.

Joe and I had planned to play our cards close to our vest and not tell her about the fake fin right away. If she had any insider info on the crime, she might accidentally tip her hand. We both liked Chuck a lot and didn't feel great about doubting her, but we couldn't ignore the hand we'd been dealt. So far, we'd identified only one person who definitely had access to the dirt on Shaggy. Until we saw Chuck's cards, we couldn't rule her out as the joker behind the blackmail.

"If someone's trying to extort money from one of my members, then I'll be the one to handle it. The poker club has a strict code, and if someone broke it, then I'll break them." Chuck pulled her wooden oar from under the bar and smacked it down on the counter. "Poor Shaggy. He really does have the worst luck."

"It's not just Shaggy they're taking advantage of, and there's more than money at stake," I said. If Chuck knew about the fake fin, she wasn't letting on at all. "Remember that huge dorsal fin everyone saw right before Trip disappeared?"

I nodded to Joe, who took the fake fin out of his bag and threw it onto the bar. "The animal sporting it wasn't a shark. It was Shaggy."

"It was what?" Chuck gasped at the plastic replica.

She went to grab it, but Joe pulled it away before she could. "Sorry. Gotta protect the evidence, just in case."

"Just in case— Wait a second! Are you saying *I'm* a suspect?"

"More like a person of interest." I shrugged apologetically. "Someone in a secret club used insider info to manipulate Shaggy into scaring a beach full of people into thinking they'd seen a shark. And that secret club has your name on it. We can't clear you until we find out who else knew about Shaggy's poker losses."

"First of all, it's not my name on Chuck's Poker Club. It's my dad's. This game has been going for decades." She pointed to an old, faded photograph of her dad with his arms around a bunch of buddies. "You know I want to help you. Especially if this has anything to do with finding Trip. I'm the one who hired you in the first place! But people trusted my dad to keep their identities a secret, and now they trust me. And what happened to Shaggy is exactly why. Sure, Lookout's elites may drop in after-hours once a week to blow off steam and have a little fun. And sure, they occasionally wager large sums of money and other sundry items—cars, boats, the deeds to their houses. It's not the kind of thing folks want getting out to the rest of the community, you know? But the only reason it works is because we keep the game a secret. How am I supposed to expect anyone else to keep Chuck's first rule if Chuck can't keep Chuck's first rule?"

Her reason for keeping quiet wasn't doing our investigation much good, but she had a point.

"Second of all," Chuck continued, "I don't know how much a membership list would help you, anyway. It's a large club. We run tournament-style games with multiple tables, and different people drop in every week."

"You said the town's elites. That can't be too many people," I pointed out, hoping to get her to narrow the suspect list down.

Chuck laughed. "You've met a bunch of the locals. 'Elite' is a relative term. Basically, the club is open to business owners and town officials. Lookout is a small town, so that's probably about a quarter of our citizens. Just about all of them come by to play a hand or twenty at some point. For all his good luck charms, Shaggy usually walks out with less than he walked in with. It's not much of a secret among the members."

"Can you think of anyone with something to gain by

getting Shaggy to scare the town with the fake shark sighting?" I asked, hoping to open up a more productive line of inquiry without divulging the theories Joe and I had discussed.

"You don't think Shaggy wearing that fin has something to do with the shark attack on Trip, do you? That doesn't make any sense. How would you fake something like that? Pictures of her paddleboard were all over the news. Even the scientists confirmed it was a tiger shark that tried to eat it."

"We were hoping talking to you would help us piece it together," Joe admitted. "The timing's suspicious to the max, but we know it wasn't a plastic shark that bit Trip's board, and we're still trying to figure out the connection."

Chuck had mentioned that her dad had started Chuck's Poker Club. When I took a closer look at the photos covering the cluttered walls, I noticed he was in a lot of them, usually grinning with his arm around one of his customers. With their matching big brown eyes, the resemblance between Chucks Senior and Junior was impossible to miss, especially in the older photos higher up on the wall, which must have been taken when Chuck Senior was around his daughter's current age.

I was checking out the pictures, only half paying attention while my brain searched for answers, when I noticed one photo near the ceiling at the far end of the bar. But it wasn't Chuck Senior or the customer he was smiling next to that caught my eye. It was the paddleboard hanging on the wall in the picture's background.

Chuck Senior hadn't only been the first Chuck, he'd also been the first Lookout resident to have his board bitten by a shark.

"Is that the board your dad was attacked on?" I asked, pointing up at the photo. I couldn't make out much detail from my seat, but based on the chunk missing from the board in the photo, I had a hunch I knew the answer.

Chuck seemed confused by my question, but then she followed my finger and smiled affectionately. "Sure is. My dad loved that thing. He probably told the story a thousand times."

Unlike EEE's brightly painted blue-and-green board, this one had a plain off-white finish. Apparently, Chuck Senior's shark chomped down on the back of his board too. That wasn't surprising. Like Cap had said, large sharks are often ambush hunters.

"That picture looks like it was taken right here in the bar," Joe observed, shifting his gaze from the photo to the board-less wall behind Chuck Junior. "How come the board's not hanging up anymore? Seems like it would be a big crowd pleaser."

Chuck winced as if the question had made her uncomfortable.

"Well, it used to be . . . but I kind of lost it in a poker game a few years back." She looked up guiltily at her dad's picture. "Sorry, Pop. I had kings over tens, and I was sure Boothby was bluffing."

"You lost your dad's paddleboard to Mayor Boothby?" Joe blurted before I had a chance.

"He was just Councilman Boothby when it happened, but yeah. The pompous clown always was lucky at cards. He had four queens. I'm still not convinced he didn't cheat."

I was a lot less concerned with her hand than with the guy who won that pot. Boothby was the person who probably benefited most from Lookout's recent shark frenzy. The same guy who had just used a shark-bitten paddleboard to justify a politically motivated shark hunt also just happened to be the owner of the only other shark-bitten paddleboard in the town's history? Chuck had said the guy was lucky, but how many odds could one opportunistic political vulture defy? Or was somebody stacking the deck?

I stared at the tiny bitten board in the background of Chuck Senior's picture. Sure, bites to the rear of a board aren't unusual for attacks when they do happen, and this one was a totally different color from the fancily painted one EEE had been riding, but still—

I hopped out of my seat and onto the bar.

"Hey! Get off there! I just cleaned that!" Chuck yelled as I reached up to pull down the photograph.

The paddleboard was out of focus, but the similarity between the two bites was eerie. I wasn't an expert on stand-up boards, but like Trip's, Chuck Senior's board was an older vintage model that looked a little different from the ones they rented on the beach nowadays. And the location of the bite . . . My detective senses were tingling, but I had to be sure.

"Do you have plastic wrap and a pen or a Sharpie?" I asked, climbing down from the bar.

"You'd better not plan on drawing all over my photo," Chuck warned.

"Good thinking, bro!" Joe said. "Not a mark, Chuck. We promise."

Chuck eyed us skeptically as she placed a roll of cling wrap and a fine-tipped marker on the bar in front of us. I tore off a piece of plastic, laid it over the glass frame, and then carefully traced the outline of the board, bite mark included. While I did that, Joe pulled up a picture on his phone from one of the news websites showing the board that had washed up yesterday. I peeled the plastic wrap with the board's outline off the photograph and laid it over the screen of Joe's phone. Joe took over the operation, using his fingers to zoom in on the board until the picture was the same size as the outline I'd traced.

They weren't just the same size and shape, though. The bite marks on the board Dougie found yesterday lined up identically with the one Chuck's dad had been attacked on thirty years before.

"Whoa, that's either an uncanny coincidence . . ." Chuck trailed off as she tried to process what she was seeing.

But I'd already come to the same conclusion. "Or that's the same board!"

FRAMED 10

"THE SHARK WAS FRAMED!" I SHOUTED.

Frank looked up from the perfectly aligned paddleboards on the screen of my phone. "The Shark Lab break-in today wasn't just about shark-hating vandals causing trouble. Whoever stole that paddleboard must have known what we'd discover if we had a chance to examine it closely enough."

"That it's not Trip's board," I clarified. "It's just been repainted to look like it. I don't know where her real board is, but the one Dougie found isn't it." I looked up at Chuck. "The one that washed up yesterday is your dad's."

"But if you're right . . . ," Chuck said slowly.

"The shark attack on Dr. Edwards was faked," I finished. "Just like the shark fin we thought we saw right before she disappeared. Whoever blackmailed Shaggy into wearing the fake fin timed it precisely so everyone would assume it was the same shark that attacked her. It worked like a charm, too. Even before Dougie found the board, half the town was assuming the worst. Then when everyone saw what they thought was Trip's board with a chunk torn out, it was the nail in the shark's coffin," Frank said.

"Embedding a fresh tiger shark tooth in the bite mark to make it look new was a nice touch," I added. Just thinking about it made me gnash *my* teeth. The perp had everyone believing tiger sharks were the monsters. The real monster was the person who might very well have sacrificed a protected shark so they could use its tooth to frame its brothers and sisters as bloodthirsty killers. We'd seen frame jobs before, but this one was even worse because the fall guys couldn't speak up to defend themselves. "Whoever did this used Lookout's biggest shark advocate to depict sharks as woman-eaters. It's downright devious."

"But if it wasn't a real shark attack, that means Trip could still be okay!" Chuck said.

Frank looked less optimistic. "I sure hope so. At least we know she wasn't eaten by a tiger shark. That doesn't mean she isn't still in danger, though."

"But if a shark didn't get Trip, who did? And"—Chuck gulped—"what happened to her?"

Frank and I had both heard Dr. Edwards scream out from the fog. The prospects didn't seem good.

"Whatever happened, I'm guessing it's a human predator we're looking for," I said. "The coastline takes a blind curve once you get past the pier, so even without the fog to give them cover, it would have been possible for someone to grab her without being seen from the shore."

"Okay, so we know our perp has arms instead of fins, but we need to narrow the list of suspects down further," Frank said. "By my count, there are two other people who we know for sure have recently come into contact with Chuck's dad's paddleboard. The guy who owns it—"

"Mayor Boothby," I spat.

"And the guy who found it."

"You think Dougie had something to do with this?" Chuck waved the suggestion off. "He's one of the sweetest guys around, and he's known Trip forever."

"Dougie finding the board washed up on the beach doesn't prove anything," Frank said. "But combine that with the fact that he was the first one on the scene after the fake fin was spotted, and the timing all starts to look suspicious."

"Isn't he the one who wanted to go looking for Trip right away, though? Why would he want to help her if he was the one who hurt her?" I argued.

"He could have been creating an alibi. We already know the perp had Shaggy doing their bidding. We don't know how many other players they've involved. The question is, did Dougie have the lowdown on Shaggy's poker losses so he could blackmail him?"

Chuck sighed. "I can't tell you if he's a member of the club, but I will say that Dougie is a professional fisherman with his own small business."

"Thanks, Chuck," I said. She'd told us earlier that the club included just about every business owner in town, so her hint was as good as a yes. Dougie had also said something when we first met about everyone having an open tab at Chuck's. That made a lot more sense in light of the poker game.

"I say we save Danger Dougie for later and go after the biggest fish first," Frank suggested. "You already let the catfish out of the bag about Boothby being in on the poker games and him winning your dad's board. He probably knows all about Shaggy's gambling woes."

"Not to mention that his whole new campaign platform is based on everyone believing a shark attacked Trip," I said.

I'd originally pegged Mayor Boothby as an opportunist taking advantage of tragedy to help himself politically, but maybe I hadn't given the guy enough credit. Maybe he hadn't just taken advantage of it—maybe he'd masterminded it!

Frank and I stepped out of Chuck's Shuck Shack into a muggy, drizzly night. Wind whipped the palm trees, and thunder rumbled in the distance. Our destination: a houseboat docked at the far end of the marina, where Chuck told us the mayor lived. We didn't bother to call ahead.

"I'd have figured the mayor would live in a fancier place

than this," Frank said as we walked down the dock toward his floating front door.

The boat was basically a one-story wooden rectangle in need of a paint job and at least one new window. Plywood covered the hole. The blinds were drawn on the others, though we could see the flicker of a TV, so we knew someone was home. The choppy water matched the dreary sky, and with a swift current tugging on the ropes mooring the houseboat to the dock, we watched our step climbing onto the deck at the houseboat's stern. There were a couple of lounge chairs set up next to a charcoal grill and a pair of paddleboards strapped to the side of the main cabin, but these were newer models without bite marks.

I knocked on the door. We heard the latch unlock a minute later. The door cracked open a sliver, and then Mayor Boothby's face peered out from behind a security chain.

"What's all this about? Do you know what time it is?" He looked at us like he had trouble placing our faces. "You're the boys who were hanging out at Chuck's place the other night? The ones who mouthed off at my town meeting?"

"That's us. Frank and Joe Hardy, shark conservationist private detectives at your service," said Frank.

The mayor recoiled, which I'm pretty sure was what Frank had in mind. "Did you say 'private detectives'? But you're teenagers."

"Yup!" I said, giving him my best boyish grin. "We take on all kinds of cases. Stolen lunch money, missing kittens, conspiracy, fraud, blackmail, criminal malfeasance. You know, the normal kid stuff."

"And right now, we're hot on the trail of a missing paddleboard and thought a civic-minded public servant like yourself might be interested in helping us find it," Frank said.

The mayor's eyes widened. "Did you say 'paddleboard'?"

"This one's just your average vintage model. Normal size. Used to be off-white, but someone painted it bright blue and green. Large shark-bite-shaped piece ripped out of the back. Nothing special. Have you seen it?"

The door slammed in our faces. "I have no idea what you're talking about! Go away!" Mayor Boothby shouted from the other side.

"Sorry, mayor dude. Not gonna happen," I called through the door. "You can either let us in to talk privately, or we can stand out here making a scene until your neighbors start dropping by to find out what all the fuss is about."

"I'm sure your voters would love to hear our theories about your involvement in another scandal," Frank added.

That did it. The chain unclicked, the door swung open, and the mayor waved us inside. He poked his head out to make sure no one was looking, before slamming the door again.

"I'm quite sure I have no idea what you're talking about, but I'd be derelict in my duties as mayor if I allowed you to stand outside causing a public disturbance," he said, smoothing his pajamas in an attempt to make himself look more formal. "Now go on with whatever you have to say so *I* can go on with my evening. I'm a very busy man, and I have important public policy documents to review before bed."

He saw me eyeing the game show playing on the TV behind him and quickly hurried over to turn it off.

The inside of the houseboat was as ramshackle as the exterior. There was stuff everywhere, some of it tossed carelessly in piles, some of it neatly organized. From the looks of the broom leaning against the pile of garbage bags by the door, the mayor was in the middle of a much-needed cleanup.

"So about that public policy," Frank said.

"And the dereliction of duty," I threw in.

"A source tells us you're the proud owner of the last paddleboard to have a bite taken out of it by a shark thirty years ago," Frank went on.

"Oh, that's what all this is about." Boothby giggled nervously. "Why, yes, I used to own old Chuck's paddleboard. It was given to me by his daughter—"

"And by 'given to,' you mean you won it in an illegal poker game?" Frank put his hands on his hips.

"The type of high-stakes game where an unscrupulous player might use another's gambling habits to blackmail them into perpetrating hoaxes against an unsuspecting public?" I added with a smirk.

Boothby's face tightened and he forced an awkward

smile. "Anyway, I used to own it, as I said, but it was stolen from my boat along with a number of other personal items during a break-in last week." He pointed at the boarded-up window and gave an exasperated look around at the rest of the messy houseboat. "As you can see, I'm still cleaning up. The hooligans ransacked the entire place. I'm normally a very tidy person."

My instinct was to not trust a word Boothby said, but the state of the houseboat supported the burglary claim. The scene looked exactly like what he said it was—a neat person in the process of cleaning up a place someone else had torn apart. But if the mayor was telling the truth and the paddleboard really had been stolen, that put us right back at square one. If we were going to track down the perp who'd blackmailed Shaggy and staged the shark attack on EEE, we needed to know who had Chuck Senior's paddleboard last.

And I couldn't help feeling there was something off about the mayor's story. Just because he was telling the truth about one thing didn't mean he wasn't lying about plenty of other stuff. If we could turn up the heat a bit, he might let whatever he was trying to hide slip. Frank and I had Boothby on the hook. Now we just had to set the line.

"There sure is an epidemic of shark-bitten paddleboard theft going around Lookout," I remarked casually. "First, yours last week. Then another one with a bite in the exact same place was stolen from Shark Lab earlier today. That's some coincidence. That makes the only two shark-bitten paddleboards in Lookout's history both snatched in a week! Strange how that other board just happened to wash up onshore so soon after yours was stolen. Then it goes missing before anyone had a chance to examine it too closely."

Boothby tried hard to maintain his poker face, but I could see him squirming behind the forced smile.

"And with you getting so much political leverage for your anti-shark initiative after Dr. Edwards's disappearance at the same time too," Frank persisted. "All because of a paddleboard with a shark bite just like the one you *say* was stolen."

"I have no idea what you could possibly mean," he said. "What happened is a terrible tragedy. Terrible. But I can't even begin to image how the break-in here has anything to do with it. You know, I can't say I ever looked at old Chuck's board very closely. It was more of a conversation piece than anything else. Quite a different color, too, now that I think about it. No similarity at all, really." The mayor nodded to himself, picking up more confidence in his story as he spoke. "And, of course, everyone saw the shark swimming around before the attack. Tragic, just tragic what that awful shark did, but out of anyone's control, sadly. Why, it never occurred to me in a million years that someone might paint my board to look like Trip's in order to stage an attack like that. The very idea is just preposterous. Now, if you'll just—" Boothby paused when he saw our matching *gotcha* grins. "What?"

"Who said anything about the attack being staged?" asked Frank, pinning the mayor with his gaze.

"Y-you did?" the mayor asked hopefully, turning a shade paler.

"Nope. We just said it was all very strange. You're the one who suggested that someone painted your board to look like Trip's." I could see Boothby sweating now.

"That's not . . . But you . . . I didn't . . . You . . . You're putting words in my mouth!" The mayor's fumbling was music to my ears—the sweet sound of a witness cracking.

"It's funny, but now that you mention the board being painted, we have photographic evidence that the attack was staged and your board was swapped out for Trip's," Frank said calmly.

"You're clearly making this all up to rattle me. No one would ever believe such a patently absurd claim," Boothby sputtered.

"Let's see what your adoring public thinks when we call a press conference in front of town hall to announce our findings." I narrowed my eyes. "I don't know who else was involved in this whole setup besides Shaggy, but we've got enough to implicate you in Councilwoman Edwards's disappearance."

"No! Please, you can't! I—I didn't have anything to do with whatever happened to Trip! I swear I didn't know it was the same board. I just—" The mayor's mouth hung open as he looked frantically from us to the door. I stepped in front of it, crossing my arms and puffing out my chest in case he was thinking about making an early exit.

"You just what?" Frank demanded. "Tell us what you know about the attack now, or we tell the public our theory tomorrow."

"Well, I didn't *know* the attack on Trip was a hoax. I mean, not a hundred percent *for sure*." He paused and wiped his brow before continuing. "But I did perhaps notice that the timing of it all seemed a bit odd. And I may have *assumed* it *possibly* was a hoax. And it's *possible* I may not have told anyone about my suspicions, and just played along with the whole shark attack thing anyway."

Boothby shrugged and gave a little chuckle while Frank and I looked on in stunned silence. Had the town's own mayor really just confessed to knowing that Dr. Edwards's disappearance had been staged from the start?

CUT LOOSE 11

FRANK

"Y OU FIGURED OUT THE ATTACK WAS A hoax and went along with it anyway?" I shouted, not entirely sure I'd heard Boothby correctly the first time.

"It seemed like a reasonable idea at the time," he muttered.

"Letting the real reason for Trip's disappearance go uninvestigated seemed reasonable?" Joe shouted even louder than I had.

"I can see how that might not look like the wisest decision in retrospect, but I didn't know for certain." Boothby averted his eyes and busied himself tidying up the end table next to the couch. "Why, it would have been irresponsible of me to jump to conclusions—"

"And I don't know for certain that you hiding the truth about Dr. Edwards will sink your political career when the rest of Lookout finds out," I said, cutting him off. "But I can make a pretty good guess that this will be your last term in office if you don't spill every one of your 'conclusions' to us right now."

"Okay, okay." He held up his hands as he settled onto the edge of the couch. "I knew there was funny business going on, but it's not like I'm the one who did it. And everyone saw that one shark, so sharks *were* swimming around scaring people, even if they weren't technically eating them."

I eyed Boothby as he talked. The way he told it, he hadn't known that the "shark" everyone saw was a fake.

"Why rock the boat?" he continued. "I mean, it's terrible if something happened to Trip, but I'm the kind of positive thinker who likes to lift my community up in times of trouble. It would be wasteful not to make the best of such an opportunity. Reduce, reuse, recycle—that's what I always say! At least this way something good came from the whole thing, right?"

"You think abandoning Trip and using a lie to scare people into supporting the slaughter of innocent sharks is 'something good'?" I snarled. "I'd sure hate to see how you define something bad."

"Well, it was good for *me*, and I can't serve the public if I'm not reelected, so it's all for the greater good."

Boothby tried to go back to straightening the lamp on the end table, but Joe grabbed it away from him.

"Do you really believe this baloney, or is it just what you tell yourself to feel better about pulling fast ones on the people who vote for you?"

"The only voter he cares about is himself," I answered before Boothby had a chance. "You knowingly aided and abetted a criminal plot because it took the heat off your other scandals and benefited you politically."

"That's not true!" Boothby started, but cut himself off when he saw Joe and me glaring. He grabbed the lamp back from Joe before continuing. "Okay, fine. Maybe it's partially true, but that's not the only reason. I'm not a bad guy. I don't want anybody to get hurt, not even the sharks. Not really. I just don't want *me* to get hurt more. And they threatened to blackmail me if I said anything about the break-in."

Now we were getting somewhere.

"Who is 'they'?" I asked.

Boothby shrugged. "Whoever stole Chuck's board from me. The note said Bruce something or other, but I'm sure the name was fake."

"Quint," Joe said, catching the mayor off guard.

"You know the guy?" His voice quavered a little, and he hugged the lamp tight to his chest.

The "honorable" mayor had proven himself untrustworthy to the max, and he still hadn't fully convinced me the real blackmailer wasn't him. But he did seem genuinely surprised—and afraid. He also didn't seem to know that the dorsal fin everyone saw was a fake. Did that mean

Mayor Boothby was another unwitting accomplice like Shaggy?

"You're not the only one who got a letter," I said, curious to see whether he'd reveal anything more.

"Is that why you mentioned Shaggy before?" Boothby asked, setting the lamp back down on the end table. "I can't see him orchestrating something like this himself, and that guy really does have the worst luck. What did they make him do?"

I exchanged a glance with Joe. I was starting to suspect Boothby was on the level with us about being a pawn in the blackmailer's schemes. One thing I'd noticed about Mayor Boothby: he wasn't so much a convincing liar as an enthusiastic one. Some people are so great at deception, you never notice anything amiss. Boothby wasn't one of them. He sold his lies with bombastic stories and a knack for reading a crowd and knowing what they wanted to hear. It's a lot easier for people to believe a lie if it confirms something they're already worried about—like sharks making them unsafe. The guy was a showman. Subtle wasn't his style.

"You know that shark everyone saw swimming around?" I said. "It was a Shaggy shark."

"A who-what?" the mayor asked.

"It was Shaggy wearing a fake fin," Joe clarified.

Boothby looked impressed. "Wow, this Quint character is good. I need to hire him to be my campaign manager."

I growled. Joe picked up the lamp.

"Sorry, kidding!" The mayor held up his hands defensively. "What did they have on Shaggy, anyway?"

"Poker secrets," Joe said, putting the lamp back down. "Kinda like the ones I figure they had on you."

"Who, me? Nooooo. I don't have any secrets," Boothby said as he readjusted the lamp. "The note this Bruce left me was more of like a general threat, you know? A don't-do-this-or-else kind of thing." He wagged his finger, before sitting up straighter. "How are we going to bring this criminal to justice? That's what I want to know! In fact, I'm thinking of making it a cornerstone of my campaign. No one pulls a scam like this on my town and gets away with it!"

"Sorry, Mr. Mayor. Distraction is a tactic that's not going to work on us," I said. "Spill it. Whatever the blackmailer had on you could help us figure out their identity."

"Well, you see, it's rather sensitive. Nothing worth mentioning, really. But it is the kind of thing I'd rather not have getting out to the general voting populace, if you know what I mean."

Joe looked up at the ceiling and started counting on his fingers. "Let's see. Lying, withholding evidence, obstruction of justice, maybe accessory to kidnapping . . ."

Boothby let out a little whimper.

"We're not here to take you down, but we will if you get in the way of us finding out who the blackmailer is," I said.

"So if I tell you, you'll keep it our little secret?" Boothby asked hopefully.

"We'll consider keeping it between us as long as it doesn't endanger anyone on Lookout Key and you agree to tell us anything and everything that might help get Trip back home safely," Joe replied.

"*And* if you call off your anti-shark initiative first thing in the morning," I added.

"But I staked my whole reelection campaign on that initiative!" Boothby protested. "I can't reverse course now. People will think I'm a flip-flopper."

"So, what do you think I should wear to tomorrow's press conference, Frank?" asked Joe. "I brought a pretty snazzy Hawaiian shirt I think would look good on camera."

"I don't know, Joe, but I think I'm going to wear my new flip-flops," I replied.

"Fine. I get the point," Boothby muttered. "It's probably for the best. I didn't know how I was going to pay for all those bounties, anyway."

The wind picked up and heavy rain started pounding down on the houseboat's roof as Boothby began his confession. The current had picked up too; the boat was swaying noticeably under our feet.

"I thought about going to the police, I really did, but the thief took more than just the paddleboard. I may have had some documents that I perhaps shouldn't have had, and if anyone else were to see them, well, it might prove a little problematic with this investigation bugaboo I've been dealing with. Not that there's anything to investigate!

The whole thing's a baseless smear campaign, of course. Everyone knows I'm the most innocent mayor Lookout has ever had. But for appearances' sake, it's probably best that no one finds out I had those documents. Ever."

"And these totally insignificant documents that could sink your career were . . . ?" I prodded.

"The thing is, technically I was supposed to get rid of ownership holdings in any local businesses with matters before the town council so there wouldn't be any conflict of interest with my job as mayor. And I did, really! Sold it all! Total transparency here! But then I was on a real hot streak at the poker club one night—I was really cleaning Maxwell's clock. It's not my fault he ran out of cash and started betting stock in the development corporation he'd formed for his new resort."

"You owned a piece of the development at the center of the town council's biggest vote at the same time you were being investigated for a conflict-of-interest corruption scandal?" Joe asked. "You've got nerve. I'll give you that."

"It's not like the stock's even worth anything," Boothby said, then paused. "Well, not unless the resort gets built. Then it could be worth a *lot*. Not that I would ever let that affect my objectivity when it comes to the development's approval. No one's more objective than me!"

"That's the problem with conflicts of interest, Mayor— even if you don't use them to your advantage, they can still be used against you," I said. "By accepting that stock, you made yourself vulnerable to manipulation and got yourself blackmailed into being an accessory to a crime. And I think you may have just told us the blackmailer's purpose, too."

"I think we could have our motive, bro," Joe said, coming to the same conclusion I had. "That company's value depends on one person: Councilwoman Dr. E. Ella Edwards. With her blocking the development, the project is worth bubkes. But if she were to, say, oh, get attacked by a shark and go missing? A lot of people could make a lot of money."

"Not just the stockholders, either," I reminded him. "A lot of regular citizens expected to profit off Mangrove Palace."

"But how many regular citizens knew Mayor Objectivity here secretly owned stock in the development so that they could blackmail him?" Joe pointed out.

The houseboat dipped under my feet as I gave the question some thought. "We're back at the same dead end we hit with Shaggy. Whoever is behind all this has to be a Chuck's Poker Club insider, but which one?"

"I can name one club member who knew you had that stock," Joe said, turning back to the mayor. Boothby stared at him blankly. "The dude who gave it to you. Maxwell."

"Huh," the mayor muttered.

"And Maxwell's savvy. I wouldn't be surprised if he ran through his cash and started losing stock on purpose. The more business leaders who had something to gain financially from Mangrove Palace's success, the more allies he'd have in his fight to get the development approved."

Joe nodded. "And the more ammunition he'd have to manipulate them."

"I did clean up with some pretty weak hands a couple weeks back," the mayor said, mulling over the prospect that he'd been allowed to win, then shaking it off just as quickly. "I prefer to think it was my intimidating self-confidence and preternatural gift for bluffing."

Joe rolled his eyes. "I don't think you're the town's only bluff artist. Maxwell talked a good game about supporting the decision to postpone the vote when we confronted him. That doesn't change the fact that he's the Lookout resident with the biggest stake in the development's approval. He benefits the most from Trip's disappearance."

"There are two prerequisites for our suspect," I said. "Access to the blackmail intel and a strong motive to want Trip out of the picture. Maxwell has them both."

Boothby was about to say something when the houseboat lurched violently to the side, sending him tumbling out of his seat. I barely managed to keep my footing, while Joe grabbed on to the end table to stop himself from falling. Boothby's lamp didn't fare as well. It dropped to the floor with a crash.

"Sorry!" Joe said.

"Talk about a shaky foundation!" I yelped as the boat dipped again. "Is it supposed to do this?"

Boothby ran over to the window and yanked up the blinds. He gasped.

"What's wrong?" Joe yelled, but the mayor appeared too shocked to reply.

We found out why when we ran to the window to see what had him so flustered.

It seemed we had a more immediate problem than identifying the blackmailer. The houseboat was being swept out to sea!

BEACON OF DOOM

12

JOE

Y OU'D BETTER TURN THE ENGINE ON and get us back to the dock quick before we smash on something," I yelled at the mayor as the lights from shore grew smaller and smaller.

"It doesn't work!" Boothby yelped.

"Drop the anchor, then!" Frank shouted.

"I don't have one!"

"Then you'd better radio for help. Fast!" I shouted.

"The thief smashed the radio!"

"Uh-oh," Frank and I said in unison, tumbling across the floor as the houseboat crested a swell and dropped us not very gently on the other side.

"I'm calling 9-1-1!" I whipped out my phone and . . .

watched the little "searching for service" icon spin in help-less circles. "Or not! There's no signal!"

"We just have the one cell tower nearby, and sometimes we lose service in bad weather," Boothby informed us. "It's one of the main issues I ran on last election."

"Um, then why isn't it working?" Frank asked.

"I'm a very busy man, and the town's had other, er, priorities—" He shrieked as the houseboat suddenly tilted dangerously to starboard.

"I'm not a big fan of your priorities," I yelled. "How do you live on a houseboat and not have an anchor?"

"I had two, but the thief cut them loose when they trashed my place. The boat was moored to the dock with rope. Those knots were secure. I double-checked them myself, and I'm the best knot-tier on Lookout."

"Yeah, just like you're the most innocent and objective politician," I cracked.

"No, really. I was an Eagle Scout. I still have my knot-tying badge." He pointed proudly to a sash full of merit badge patches hanging on the wall next to an antique grappling hook.

"Huh. There it is," Frank said.

"There's no way those knots could have come undone by themselves," Boothby insisted.

That left only one other possibility.

"Someone cut us loose," I growled.

Frank ran to the other side of the boat and yanked up

the curtains just in time for us to see the boat narrowly miss smashing against a buoy. "Well, we'd better get un-loose fast or we're going to be in real trouble."

"How much realer can trouble get?" the mayor squeaked. "What do you think this is, a leisure cruise?"

I shrugged. "On the bright side, in our experience, sabotage is a good sign an investigation is on the right track."

"I don't want to be on the right track!" the mayor wailed.

"You said the engine doesn't work. Did the thief disable that, too?" I asked. I definitely wasn't a boat mechanic, but I had some experience tinkering around with motors. "Maybe it's something we can fix."

"The engine disabled itself a long time ago," Boothby answered, sinking my already flimsy plan. "This old tub is a lot more house than boat. She hasn't been seaworthy for years."

"Worthy or not, she's on the sea now," Frank said, looking out the window as the current carried us toward the peninsula south of the marina.

The eerie silhouette of Alligator Lighthouse was just barely visible through the pouring rain. I stared at the darkened little window atop the rickety structure, where an iconic beacon light should have been shining.

"Maybe if your mayoral priorities included renovating historical landmarks, there might have been someone in that lighthouse to spot us and send help."

"Humph. Everybody's a political pundit these days." Boothby crossed his arms and scowled.

His expression changed to fear a second later. "We're headed toward the lighthouse?" He leaped up and joined us by the window, then yelped. "We're doomed! The current's carrying us straight toward the reef!"

He scrambled to a bin by the door, pulled out a pair of life vests, and frantically started putting one on.

"Good thinking, Mayor," I said, holding out my hand. "Hopefully we won't need them, but I don't want to take any chances."

"I only have two," he snapped, clutching the second one to his chest.

"Joe and I can share one," Frank said.

"But what if I need a backup?" Boothby clutched the other vest even tighter.

"Bad mayor!" I glared at him. "For a second there, I thought you were looking out for someone other than yourself."

He looked guiltily at his slippers but didn't loosen his grip on the extra life vest. I did a quick scan of the cabin. Even if there had been enough vests to go around, they were still a last resort. We needed some kind of plan to keep the houseboat on the water and us out of it.

I ran out the door onto the little deck by the stern to get a better look at our surroundings. The reef was ahead to our left. The shore was to our right. Unless we got incredibly lucky, we were going to smash into one of them. In that moment, the shore seemed likely. Not so bad if it had been one of those nice, soft, sandy beaches like the one by the marina, but this one had tons of large sea-worn rocks jutting out into the surf. And just in case the view didn't look perilous enough, the mast from an old shipwreck poked out from the surf, giving me a chilling glimpse of our own fate if something didn't change fast.

"The current's carrying us toward those rocks!" I shouted.

Past them, I could see a few funky-looking mangrove trees growing out of the shallows. The twisted mounds of exposed roots that anchored them to shore looked old and gnarled enough to have survived storms a lot worse than this one.

As bleak as the situation was, something about those tangled roots made me smile.

I ran back inside shouting, "We may not have an anchor, but maybe we can borrow one!"

The mayor looked out the window at the ocean, then back at me. "Borrow one? From whom?" He buried his face in his hands. "He's cracking up under pressure! I'm cracking up under pressure! We're all going to die!"

Frank was more composed. "Hit me, Joe. What's the plan?"

"It's not you I'm going to hit," I said, reaching up to grab the grappling hook off the wall. "It's the mangroves."

The grappling hook looked like an oversize, rusty four-prong fishing hook with an equally rusty length of chain attached to it. It was easy to imagine a pirate tossing it over a ship's side to grab on to a merchant vessel before boarding and pillaging it. I wasn't sure if what I had in mind was going to be any less dangerous, but at least the trees wouldn't be shooting at us.

"Grab the end of that rope, bro!" I called, pointing out the door at the long coil on the deck.

Frank saluted, dashed outside, and returned with the rope.

"Okay, Mayor McKnotMaster," I said. "Let's see what you got. I'm going to tie one end of this rope to the grappling hook, and I need you to fasten the other end to the boat."

"Yes, sir!" The mayor must have flashed back to the Eagle Scouts, because he instantly snapped to attention, grabbed the rope, went out to the deck, and started fastening it to one of the houseboat's cleats.

"That knot's not going anywhere, and that's one campaign promise you can bank on," he declared proudly a minute later.

"How 'bout this one?" I asked, handing him the knot I'd tied to the grappling hook's chain.

He eyed it for a second before looking up. "I could do better, of course, but not a bad job for an amateur."

I took a deep breath as the houseboat swept toward the outcropping of mangroves. If I'd estimated correctly, we'd have barely enough rope. Now I just had to time my throw right.

"What now?" the mayor asked anxiously.

"Stand back and hold on," I said, clutching the rope in one hand and the hook in the other.

I had one shot at this.

I took another deep breath as I stepped out into the pouring rain, lined up the target with my eyes, wound up with my arm, and let the hook fly. We watched the hook sail toward the closest mangrove tree, then fall—right in the center of the tangled roots I'd been aiming for!

"Come on, come on." The hook rattled around, looking for purchase.

"I think it's grappled!" Frank shouted.

It was hard to make out through the rain, but I'd hit the mark, and it looked like I'd hooked on to the thicker roots like I'd meant to. Now it just had to hold.

I could feel the hook starting to slip. Then . . .

"Yes!" Frank shouted as the boat's momentum pulled the rope taut, snapping us to a sudden stop that sent all three of us tumbling onto the deck. We couldn't have been happier about it. The current was doing its best to yank us loose, but the grappling hook held. For now.

"Well done, my young protégé!" the mayor shouted.

"Now let's get off this tub before the current carries us down the drain," I said. "We're close enough to shore that the water should start getting shallow. It'll be a little dicey, but we can climb over one by one and use the rope to guide us to solid ground."

Mayor Boothby eyed the swiftly moving water apprehensively.

"I'll go first. Frank can take the rear. We'll spot you in case anything goes wrong," I reassured him.

I was just about to take the plunge when the ocean decided on a change of plans.

The current swept our tethered boat around the mangroves—and right into a surprisingly calm little cove. "Huh," said Frank. "Looks like abandoning ship will be easier than we expected."

"This spot is perfectly nestled in the curve of the peninsula to shelter it from the worst of the storm." I surveyed the terrain. A narrow channel cut its way downstream at the far end of the cove.

Boothby studied the mouth of the channel and nodded. "If I have my bearings right, that channel runs right past the lighthouse. Not much besides mangroves and gators between here and there, but there's another little wharf just down the coast on the other side."

I slapped my hand on one of the paddleboards lashed to the side of the houseboat. "Paddleboards may not be the luckiest form of transportation around here lately, but I think they might be our best shot to make it back to civilization quickly. The current here is swift enough to carry us to the wharf without us needing to paddle much, but it's not so choppy that we can't navigate it."

The mayor's apprehensive look had returned.

Frank eyed the lightning in the distance. "I don't like paddling through a storm like this either, but I don't know if staying by the boat is any safer. Even if your knots hold, the rope might not. And lightning is a risk whether we're on the boat or not. I say we head for the wharf and look for shelter along the way."

"There are only two boards, so Frank and I can ride together if you want your own," I offered the mayor, realizing he was still hogging both life vests. "I mean, unless you think you need both of those as well."

He sheepishly handed over the second life vest. Mayor Boothby had a ways to go before I would call him generous, but this was progress, at least.

"There's one upside to getting cut loose and swept down the coast," Frank said as we unlashed the paddleboards and climbed off the houseboat into the water. "Whoever did the cutting probably assumes we're out to sea and no longer a threat. With a little luck, we should be able to make it back and alert the authorities without the crook knowing."

We were on our boards, about to set off toward Alligator Lighthouse, when a flash of lightning illuminated the night sky behind the condemned landmark. All three of us froze as the image flickered in the electric light like a scene from a horror movie.

"So much for that luck, bro. I think the bad guy knows we're headed straight for his lair."

Why did I think it was the blackmailer's lair? The abandoned lighthouse wasn't all the lightning had illuminated, and it wasn't abandoned anymore. There was a silhouette in the tower window. Someone was watching us through a spyglass.

AMBUSH HUNTERS

13

FRANK

Y OU THINK THAT'S THE BLACKMAILER up there?" Mayor Boothby's voice shook as the lightning strike faded and the silhouette watching us from the lighthouse tower vanished back into the darkness.

"Everyone on Lookout knows it's condemned, right?" I said. "From what we heard, it's a death trap and strictly off-limits."

He nodded. "When I toured the site with the town council, our engineer said it shouldn't even still be standing. Some kids snuck in last year and had to be rescued by the fire department when they fell through the floor. No one's been reckless enough to trespass since."

"Until now," Joe pointed out. "If someone climbed all the

way up there in the middle of a storm to use it as a crow's nest to watch the coastline, there's got to be a good reason."

"Or a bad one," I said. "And spying on the houseboat you just cut loose would definitely count."

"If it is the perp, they could be using it as more than just a lookout." Joe squinted through the rain toward the lighthouse. "The whole search-and-rescue operation for Trip was focused on the water and the shoreline because everyone believed she'd been attacked by a shark or marooned in the storm. No one thought to look inside anywhere because no one suspected she could have been taken somewhere against her will."

"Until we started putting the pieces together. . . . If you kidnapped someone and needed a place to hide them where no one would look, the least safe place you could find might be the safest place not to be found," I concluded.

"I think we know where we're headed next, dude." Joe tightened his grip on the paddle.

"You want to go in there after them?" the mayor asked incredulously.

"We don't know what really happened to Trip, but if there's a chance she's in there and needs help, we have to take the risk. If we're right and we saw the perp, they may realize we spotted them in that lightning strike." I shuddered as I thought about what that could mean. "They might try to get rid of the evidence before we can expose them."

We were silent for a moment. We all knew the biggest piece of evidence might be Trip herself.

Joe thrust his paddle into the water, ready to propel us forward. "Let's do this."

Boothby cleared his throat conspicuously before we could push off. "Just to clarify, you want us to go into a death trap where the criminals who just tried to kill me are hiding out?" he asked doubtfully. Joe and I nodded. "Good plan! Take the fight right to them! I commend you boys on your intrepidness. I wish I could join you in your endeavor, but I mean too much to the people of Lookout to put myself at risk. It would be downright irresponsible of me. Clearly, the more heroic thing for me to do is to stay here and man the ship."

"Clearly," Joe said, unconvinced.

Boothby did at least brief us on the lay of the land by the lighthouse before we left, so I guess he wasn't entirely useless. The good news was, the banks of the channel were overgrown with enough vegetation that our approach should be concealed. There were two entrances—one at ground level and one two stories up, accessible by ladder in case the ground level was submerged in a storm surge.

The current in the channel was swift, but a whole lot less choppy than the ocean had been, and it wasn't long before we reached our final, terrifying destination. We stashed our paddleboards in the overgrowth, using the ankle leashes to secure them to a palm tree so they wouldn't take off without us. The storm was howling, and Joe and I were both soaked to the bone, but our adrenaline was pumping so high, we barely noticed.

"I don't see anyone up there," Joe whispered, peering up at the lighthouse tower from an overgrown hiding spot just a few yards away.

Thunder was booming quicker and louder, which meant more lightning setting the night sky aglow. The better for us to see by—or be seen.

Alligator Lighthouse was a six-story stone cylinder tilting precariously to the right. It had once been painted in fat red-and-white stripes like a nautical candy cane, but the paint was so faded, you could barely tell anymore. The weathered stone was cracked and battered; it looked like it had lived through a naval assault. Entire chunks were missing from the top few levels, exposing the interior to the elements. A long-ago-shattered glass roost sat at the very top. The silhouette of the huge beacon light was still visible inside. Right then, that was the only silhouette visible. Whoever had been there earlier was gone.

The entire structure was surrounded by a chain-link fence topped with barbed wire. The lighthouse was set back a ways from the breaking waves, but not so far that foam from the surging tide didn't reach past the fence. If that tide kept rising . . . It was easy to imagine why the lighthouse needed more than just a first-floor entrance.

"I don't think anyone's going to mistake this place for a playground, that's for sure," Joe whispered, taking in the numerous bright orange signs along the fence warning trespassers of both the danger and illegality of trying to get inside.

"That hasn't stopped someone from cutting a slice

through the fence with wire cutters." I wouldn't have spotted the damaged chain link if it weren't for one thing.

"The ground leading up to the gap in the fence is the only place where the seagrass is tramped down. Someone's been in and out this way recently," Joe said.

The last lightning flash brightened the surroundings long enough for us to fully take in the two entrances the mayor had described—and the fact that he'd omitted a pretty important detail.

"Looks like the decision between the main entrance and the ladder has been made for us." Joe sighed. "We'd need a crowbar and half an hour to get in through the boards covering the front door."

"Which means whoever's in there knows exactly which entrance to defend. So much for the element of surprise." I grimaced at our remaining option, two very precarious stories off the ground.

"We've been in more dangerous predicaments than this," Joe reminded me. After a moment, he added, "Okay, maybe not *more* dangerous than this, but maybe equally dangerous?"

I groaned. "Let's just get this over with before I have third thoughts. We might still have the advantage. We don't know for sure that they realize we spotted them. It could just be some random vagrant or thrill seeker anyway."

"There's only one way to find out." Joe pushed his way through the slit in the fence and dashed toward the ladder in a crouching run.

There was no turning back now. I was right behind him.

Joe hesitated at the top of the rusty iron ladder, right below an open window. I could tell it used to be secured too, but there was only one board left. The rest looked like they'd been pried off long ago. Anyone intrepid enough (great vocab word, Mayor!) could have entered. I just hoped whoever had gone in last wasn't intrepid *and* diabolical.

Holding on to the ladder with one hand, Joe carefully pulled out his cell phone and opened the camera. I might have thought it was odd if I didn't already know the surveillance trick he had in mind. As soon as he heard the next thunderclap, he raised just the lens over the window ledge and waited for the lightning to arrive. When it did, an image of the lighthouse's interior filled the screen. It lasted only a second, and we couldn't see much beyond flickering shadows, but the flash provided enough light for us to tell there was no one lurking right in front of the window, ready to ambush us.

Joe pocketed his phone and poked his head through the opening. I held my breath. And then sighed in relief as he pulled himself all the way inside.

I had just reached the window ledge when another lightning bolt illuminated the inside of the lighthouse. We'd gotten only a sliver of it through the lens of Joe's camera. This time, we saw the entire story below us.

The space was one large, open cylinder, allowing me to take in most of it from the window. A rusty iron spiral staircase with an equally rusty guardrail wound its way along the wall from the wet floor, past our window, through a rotting ceiling a couple of stories above, and presumably up to the unseen pinnacle beyond that. It looked like there might have been another floor between us and the ceiling at one point, but if it had ever existed, it had collapsed years before. The ground level below us was a damp mess of crumbling stone, rotted wood, and long-forgotten nautical junk.

Not all of it was junk, though. There were a pair of nearly matching bright blue-and-green paddleboards.

The only difference: one had a large bite taken out of it. Any doubts we'd had about this being the blackmailer's lair were gone.

I didn't have a chance to look very far above me, but what I did see definitely left an impression. I wasn't an expert on lighthouse architecture, but this one had a feature I'm pretty sure didn't come with the original design. So those metal cages shark divers use to protect themselves from great whites while filming *Shark Week* documentaries? One of them was suspended from the ceiling by a rusty metal chain. That wasn't even the most unusual part.

That would be the person trapped inside.

"Dr. Edwards!" Joe cried.

The first thing I noticed about the acclaimed shark researcher was that she had conclusively *not* been eaten by one of her subjects. While she didn't look like she was in great shape, she was very much alive. She was wearing the same board shorts and Shark Lab tee she'd had on when she disappeared into the fog two days before, only they were a lot more tattered.

I took a mental snapshot of the scene before the light faded. The cage was constructed with narrowly spaced vertical steel bars separated by a large enough horizontal opening at eye level that a diver could swim out if they had to, but a large shark couldn't swim in. Unfortunately, swimming out wasn't a thing you could do suspended in the air three stories off the ground. Had EEE wanted to, she could have climbed out, but there was nowhere for her to go. Up wasn't an option either. The chain descending from the ceiling was wrapped in barbed wire to make sure she didn't get any ideas about scrambling to freedom.

It looked like the whole setup was rigged on some kind of pulley system to raise and lower the cage, but I couldn't see where it originated. A bucket hung above the cage, attached to a thin strand of fishing line. The kidnapper must have used it to lower food and water down to Dr. Edwards.

Just before the light went out, Trip saw us, and her eyes went wide. She was pointing above us and yelling, but between the rain, thunder, and crashing waves, I couldn't make out what she was saying.

We were thrown back into darkness, but another bolt illuminated the crumbling lighthouse's interior—along with the wild-eyed, tattooed shark hunter charging down the stairs at Joe with a harpoon!

DOWNWARD SPIRAL

14

JOE

THREE THINGS FLASHED BEFORE MY eyes in the span of a few seconds: our no-longer-missing marine biologist dangling from the ceiling in a cage; Captain Diamond about to impale me with a harpoon; and my life, because Captain Diamond was about to impale me with a harpoon!

The rickety spiral staircase shook with each of Diamond's murderous steps, threatening to tear the whole thing loose from the wall. I had only a few seconds to act, and just as few options: jump over the side and drop two whole stories to the ground below; charge up the stairs toward a harpooner with a high-ground advantage; dive back out the window and hope I didn't somehow knock both Frank and me off the ladder; or retreat down the stairs as quickly as I could and hope for a miracle.

I opted for the only one that didn't involve almost certain doom. I ran down.

Diamond had two big advantages: a running start and a frighteningly long, pointy implement to close the distance.

But it turned out I had an unseen advantage of my own. Frank!

Diamond hadn't realized there was someone else waiting to climb in the window. Frank hurled himself through the frame the instant Diamond stepped in front of it, throwing his body into the crazed captain before he could reach me. Not that I saw it happen. I wasn't about to stop and turn around with that harpoon ready to make a Joe kebab, but I was close enough to hear Frank's war cry, Diamond's grunt, and an unidentified metallic screeching.

I figured out what the sound was soon enough—the rail tearing away from the narrow staircase, followed by me tearing away with it!

The metal steps twisted under my feet, throwing me off-balance. A second earlier, the guardrail would have caught me, but Frank's and Diamond's combined weight had torn it loose. I was airborne for only a split second before managing to catch hold of the detached rail. The metal dug into my palms and the rail gave another screech. This time it held, still attached higher up the staircase. Unfortunately, I was floating in the air a few feet away from the closest step.

When I looked up, I realized I wasn't the only one dangling. The shaft of Captain Diamond's harpoon had gotten wedged between the metal steps, and he was clinging to it with both hands.

If you counted EEE suspended from the ceiling in the shark cage, that made three out of four lighthouse occupants dangling a full twenty feet or more off the ground. Even if someone could survive a drop from that height, all the jagged, rusty debris cluttering the floor wasn't going to make for a very cushy landing.

Thankfully, my bro still had something somewhat solid under him, at least for the moment. The ancient bolts fastening the spiral staircase to the crumbling stone wall looked like they might pull free at any moment. The wind had shifted, sending sheets of rain whipping in through the open window, turning the stairs into a mini indoor waterfall. Like they weren't dangerous enough already!

Frank left Diamond grunting and shouting as the shark hunter tried to use his grip on the harpoon to pull himself back up. The storm had only gotten louder, and I couldn't make out what Diamond was saying, but it didn't take a detective to deduce that it wasn't friendly.

"Give me your hand, Joe!" Frank shouted, reaching out to me with one hand while hugging the wall behind him with the other to keep from slipping off and following me over the side.

"I don't think I can without losing my grip or pulling you

down," I said with a grunt of my own. "I'm gonna try to swing my feet over and maybe you can pull me up."

The rail groaned angrily, pulling farther away from the wall, and I could tell from the worry lines on Frank's forehead that he wasn't any more confident my plan would work than I was. I almost made it on my second attempt, only to have my feet fall a few inches short of Frank's grasp. I didn't know how much more swinging either my palms or the free-floating railing could take, but I didn't have any choice except to keep trying. The lightning was coming fast and furious, flashing us in and out of darkness, which didn't make the job any easier.

I was gearing up for another attempt when I saw Frank look up toward the window. My first thought was that Diamond had made it back onto the stairs, but I knew that wasn't the case when I saw the lines on Frank's forehead melt away with relief.

"Quick! Help me pull Joe up!" he yelled up at the window. "Diamond's been holding Trip captive. He tried to kill us when we tracked him back here!"

I couldn't see who Frank was calling to, but there was lantern light shining through the window; it was obvious that Frank recognized the person as a friend. I thought Mayor Boothby might have caught the bravery bug and followed us after all, but it was a different Lookout resident who climbed through the window, carrying a small camping lantern.

Cap! I cheered in my brain, afraid that shouting out,

holding on to the rail, and trying to swing all at once might be more than my straining body could handle. The captain of the R/V *Sally* assessed the situation quickly, looking from Frank to me to his archenemy, Captain Diamond, struggling to hold on to the harpoon.

Cap wasn't the only member of Shark Lab that I could make out. Trip was gripping the bars of the dangling shark cage.

But the expression on her face wasn't hope, like I expected. It was fury.

Cap looked at Frank with the same sick-to-his-stomach face he'd been wearing since Trip first went missing. "I'm sorry I didn't take you boys seriously when you said you were detectives. I would have tried harder to make you go home. I didn't want you to get hurt."

He reached out his hand, only it wasn't me he was reaching out to help. It was Diamond.

TOO MANY CAPTAINS IN THE KITCHEN

15

FRANK

THE INSTANT I SAW CAP TURN AWAY to reach for EEE's captor, I realized Joe and I had overlooked an important detail earlier when we'd first spotted the silhouette watching us from the lighthouse: whoever was up in that tower couldn't have had time to cut the houseboat loose and make it back down the coast to the lighthouse to spy on us. They had to be working with a partner.

But even if we had realized that the houseboat saboteur was still unaccounted for, the last person anyone on Lookout would have expected to team up with the self-proclaimed "Shark Hunter" was his shark-loving rival.

That wasn't even the most devious part about it, though.

I looked up past "Cap" Rogers, the proud captain of a

research vessel dedicated to shark conservation, to Dr. "Triple E" Edwards imprisoned in the shark cage suspended above his head. If I had it worked out right this time, Trip's Shark Lab research partner was also one of her captors. Trip's words were drowned out by the storm, but the way she was banging on the bars of the cage and screaming at him seemed to confirm it.

I growled in Cap's direction, but bringing him to justice was going to have to wait. Joe was still in danger. Thankfully, while Cap was helping his ex-enemy climb back onto the spiral staircase, Joe had kept swinging. This time, he made it close enough for me to grab him around the ankles. And not a second too soon. The force of his swing finally yanked the railing free. We teetered on the step's edge. A wrong breeze could have plunged us to the ground and turned us into chum. I managed to regain my balance and pull us both against the temporary safety of the lighthouse wall.

A glance up the stairs made it clear that we weren't the only team that had gotten back together. Diamond was solidly on the staircase, and it didn't look like he was going to ask us to stay for a friendly chat about the weather.

"Perfect," Joe groaned, his arms hanging limply by his sides. "Safe again just in time to not be safe again."

The good news was that the harpoon hadn't made it back onto the stairs with Diamond. He sat weaponless beside Cap, catching his breath, massaging his own tired, tattooed arms. Seeing the shark hanging by its tail on each arm made me even more heated. It was obvious that Joe and I weren't the only angry ones. Trip was still yelling down, but the wind, rain, and surf continued to overpower her calls.

With each new wave, the ocean's roar seemed to get louder. The entire lighthouse felt like it was shaking, like the next crash might bring the whole place down.

Cap's lantern must have been intentionally dimmed to keep anyone in the distance from seeing a light where it shouldn't have been. The beam didn't reach the ground floor, so it wasn't until the next lightning strike that I saw that the stone floor wasn't just wet anymore—it was under a few inches of water. When the next wave slammed into the lighthouse, I could practically taste the sea spray from two stories up.

"How could you betray Shark Lab like this?" I yelled.

"I was trying to *save* Shark Lab!" Cap yelled back.

Diamond laughed bitterly. "You was trying to get paid, just like me, you hypocrite."

Cap ignored him. "I was trying to fund our research. Without the R/V, the lab is landlocked. We can't do any of our most important fieldwork without *Sally*. This was the only way I could make sure the lab thrived."

"You keep telling yourself that, Cap'n Crunch," Diamond said, sneering. Clearly, being partners in crime didn't make the captains BFFs. "You being a spineless jellyfish is about the only thing that loudmouth scientist and I done agree on. If she hadn't lost her voice that first night, I mighta cut my own ears off just for some peace and quiet."

That explained why we hadn't been able to hear Trip screaming. It was reassuring to know she'd given her kidnappers an earful. Not having a voice didn't seem to slow her down much either. She continued to shout silently and pound on the bars, making the whole cage sway.

The captains' bickering revealed that money was part of the motive, and Cap's insistence that he was trying to fund the lab's research revealed another. But I couldn't quite put the pieces together. Cap had told us he was struggling to make payments on the R/V and that Shark Lab didn't have a lot of money in reserve. Apparently, things were even worse than he'd let on. But how could kidnapping the person who ran the organization he claimed he was trying to help solve that? It wasn't like they could hold her for ransom.

"How does putting the head of Shark Lab in a cage help Shark Lab?" I shouted at Cap. "Whoever's paying you, it can't be worth it."

"I don't much like the sound of these guppies whining either." Diamond shook the kinks out of his arms and climbed to his feet. "Now let's stop yammering and do what's gotta be done."

Cap grabbed him by the shoulder. "Hold on a second. You're not saying we should actually harm them?"

Diamond brushed away Cap's hand and stalked forward. "I'm a man of action, Crunchy. I'm done saying. I'm just doing."

"They're only kids!" Cap protested.

"Sharks, kids. Don't make no difference to me." Diamond shot a glance up at EEE. "They've seen the endangered fish we been keeping in that live tank up there. You think we let them go, they ain't gonna go squawking straight to the fuzz?"

"Well—well, yes. But still, that's not . . . you can't just . . . I mean—" Cap fumbled to mount a defense.

"Uh-huh." Diamond grunted dismissively, cracking his knuckles to display the words SHARK HUNTER tattooed across the backs of his hands. "Time to do a little hunting."

"Here we go again, bro." Joe sighed, climbing back to his feet and cracking his own untattooed knuckles.

If Diamond was intimidated, he sure didn't show it. The way I figured it, we could stand our ground on the slippery, narrow staircase or let him chase us down to the boarded-up, flooding ground floor. Neither option one nor option two sounded like a lot of fun.

Before I had a chance to pick, the lighthouse decided it liked option three better. There was another metallic screech as Diamond took his next step. The screech was quickly joined by the shark hunter's own shriek as the section of steps in front of him tore out of the wall. He reached back frantically, fumbling to grab hold of Cap before he could drop to the ground floor below along with the falling chunk of metal. Whether Cap wanted to help his frenemy or not, this time he didn't have a choice. He yanked himself backward with Diamond clinging on, to keep his falling accomplice from pulling them both over.

There was now a large gap in the steps separating us from the bad guys. The good news was they couldn't easily reach us. The bad news was we were trapped on a section of steps leading down to a flooding chamber with no exit.

Diamond got back to his feet and stared at the gap like he was measuring it up to see if he could leap across, then appeared to think better of it. He pounded a frustrated fist against the wall instead, smashing a dent in the fragile stone.

"This is your fault," he snarled at Cap. "We shoulda gotten rid of the evidence and cleared this place out soon as that vote was postponed, like I wanted."

"She's not evidence!" Cap shouted back. "She's my friend!"

"You probably shoulda thought of that before you agreed to let me snatch her," Diamond countered.

"Yeah, I don't know about Lookout, but in Bayport, kidnapping isn't something decent people usually do to people they consider friends," Joe said. "Or anyone really, for that matter."

"It was only supposed to be for a day or two," Cap explained, as if that made it any better. "I thought she'd come around."

"So you had Diamond do the dirty work of abducting Trip while you were onshore with us creating your alibi," I said, filling in the blanks.

I didn't know if Trip could hear us, but the angry pounding on the floor of the cage above us grew more intense.

"She put up as much of a fight as some of the sharks I've landed too." Diamond looked up at the cage. He sounded kind of impressed. "If we hadn't lucked out with the weather and that fog hadn't rolled in just in time so I could creep right up on her in the rowboat, she might have been the one that got away. Everyone knows she takes her little paddleboard out to see the cutesy-wootsy little baby sharks just about the same time every day, and can't nobody see what's going on in that little blind curve along the coast. Good thing, too, 'cause it took me a lot longer than I liked to land her and get her strung up."

"Not so long that you couldn't head over to Chuck's to put in an appearance and make sure you were accounted for," I said. "Picking a fight with Cap so no one would have any idea you two were a lot cozier than you seem was a nice extra touch."

"Aw, you hear that, skipper? The kids think we're cozy." Diamond ruffled Cap's hair in a not-so-playful way.

Cap shoved his hand away. "I never should have let you talk me into this."

"You practically jumped right into my arms when I told you how much we could make out for if we played our cards right," Diamond said.

"Who was paying you?" I asked. Cap and Diamond's bickering had given Joe and me a lot of the puzzle, but there were still key pieces missing. Who could and would fund an operation to take Dr. Edwards out of the picture? I could think of only one name with both the means and the motive. "Was it Maxwell?"

When Cap winced and looked away, I thought I had my answer.

Diamond just laughed. "That fat cat ain't got nothing but everything to do with this."

"Your grammar is as big a mystery as this case," said Joe. "Maxwell has nothing to do with it? Or everything to do with it? Which one is it?"

"Little of both," Diamond replied, clearly enjoying whatever game he was playing. "He don't know it, but we're about to make him richer right along with us."

"Is this about the stock you stole from Boothby?" I asked, trying to figure out something Maxwell wouldn't know about that might still benefit him along with the kidnappers. Trip not being around to cast her vote against his resort would certainly count, and once you added the skyrocketing value of the Mangrove Palace Development Corporation stock, you had the financial part of the equation as well. But when the mayor had said he'd won the stock from Maxwell, I hadn't been envisioning the small fortune Cap and Diamond seemed to be talking about. "How much did the mayor win?"

"Oh, a nice hunk," Diamond said. "But he ain't won half as much as your man Cap."

Joe and I both gawked at the R/V *Sally*'s captain.

"I meant to burn it," Cap said guiltily. "That's what Trip did with hers."

"You and Trip are both members of Chuck's Poker Club?" I asked. Now that I thought about it, I understood that the Shark Lab–founding councilwoman qualified for membership, but it hadn't occurred to me that she might have been among the card sharks at Lookout's underground gambling den.

Cap nodded sadly. "That's where Trip and I first became friends and decided to partner my *Sally* up with Shark Lab. She usually goes more for the social scene than the games, but she's been playing poker since she was a kid, so she knows her way around a deck of cards. She couldn't wait to take some of the air out of Maxwell's sails."

Small chunks of plaster tumbled down onto the stairs from the ceiling above as Trip shook the cage in frustration. Diamond brushed some off his shoulder without bothering to look up.

"I was fuming that night at Chuck's. Half the room done scored that stock off Maxwell, and I couldn't win a single hand," Diamond griped. "I wanted to get in on that action too."

"Let me guess. Everyone who won stock that night was either dead set against his development or had the power to influence the vote," I said.

Diamond scratched his beard for a second. "Come to think of it, yeah."

"We figured Maxwell was too savvy to lose that stock by accident. He knew that by doling out shares, he was winning over friends and softening enemies without even having to say a word," Joe explained.

The idea that he'd been manipulated by Maxwell seemed to hit Cap hard. The developer might not have paid him off directly or had any idea just how much it would influence the *Sally*'s captain, but he'd planted the seed by putting that stock in Cap's hands. By giving Cap a financial stake in his development corporation, Maxwell also gave Cap a reason to want Mangrove Palace to get built. Cap had been one of the development's biggest opponents, and without the prospect of a big payday, he never would have betrayed Shark Lab or Trip.

"Too bad y'all figured out about Boothby," Diamond said. "Soon as I seen him ogling the bundle of stock he won, I knew that crook be ripe for the picking. Between us giving that old bitten board of his a paint job, and everybody seeing that fin I done made Shaggy wear, it was a lock the whole town would pin it on that make-believe shark."

"Shaggy and the mayor couldn't expose any suspicions they had without exposing their own skeletons in the process, but what about Dougie?" I asked. "Did you blackmail him, too?"

"Dougie wasn't involved. He always visits the same spots every morning, so I planted the board where I knew he'd find it," Cap confessed.

"No wonder you were so tired this morning," Joe said. "Between that, terrorizing Trip, and staying up to self-sabotage the motorboat with chum to try to scare us off, you must have had a few late nights."

Cap didn't reply, but I could see the shame on his face in the lantern light.

"Except for Cap botching the scaring-y'all-off part, the whole operation started out smooth sailing," Diamond said, sounding impressed with himself. "I gotta say, though, I didn't expect Mr. Mayor to hand me an early birthday present like he done. That shark initiative of his was a heck of an added bonus."

"Don't get too excited," I said. "The mayor's ending it first thing in the morning."

Diamond shrugged. "Can't be having everything, I guess. It was worth it, though, just to see Cap's face when I told Trip here what he accidentally done to them precious sharks of hers along with kidnapping her."

Cap bit down on his lip. "This isn't how I wanted it to go. I didn't want the sharks, or anyone else, to get hurt."

"Then you probably shouldn't have framed a shark for your friend's disappearance and stuck her in a cage in an abandoned lighthouse." Joe pointed up at the shark cage swaying from the ceiling. It was swaying because the irate prisoner inside was pounding relentlessly on the bars. "I may not be superstitious like Shaggy, but that's usually not a winning recipe for good karma."

"He's got a point there, ol' buddy," Diamond said with a yawn. "Now, as much as I haven't enjoyed talking with y'all, I wanna get this over with while we still got some cover from the storm." He looked at the gap in the stairs preventing us from reaching him—or the window, which also happened to be our only escape route. "Since it ain't looking like you boys be going nowhere no time soon, I'm just gonna mosey on upstairs while y'all chat and get my speargun. I'll be back in two shakes of a shark's tail to bid you a safe voyage into the beyond."

He vanished into the darkness.

"I'm so sorry you boys got dragged into this," Cap said. Hunched over on the steps and drenched from the storm, he looked sorry too.

"Apology not accepted." I scowled, wiping rainwater out of my face. Whatever roof was left on the lighthouse, it wasn't doing its job. Though not as bad as the downpour assaulting the island outside, steady streams of water dripped from above and ran down the walls. Lightning glimmered off the water flooding into the ground level. The front door had been boarded up from the inside, as well as the exterior. Even if we'd wanted to wade into the water to try to break our way out, I doubted we'd make much headway before Diamond returned. Besides, leaving EEE trapped with him wasn't an option.

"I thought Trip would come around if she gave me a chance to really explain," Cap said.

"You know, there are more socially acceptable forms of persuasion than kidnapping, dude," Joe told him.

"I tried to reason with her first," Cap insisted. "She wouldn't take the donations Maxwell tried to give us, and if she voted down the Mangrove Palace development, the stock I'd won would have been worthless. Shark Lab was running out of money to keep up with the *Sally*'s overhead costs and to pay the crew. We couldn't afford to turn money down because its source didn't line up exactly with our principles. Without a big infusion of cash, the whole lab risked going under. It's been hard enough staying on top of *Sally*'s bank loan payments even with the Shark Lab contract. Without it—I couldn't let the bank take her away from me!"

"It all keeps coming back to what's best for you," I said. "What about Trip and Shark Lab? What about the sharks? You were the loudest voice speaking out *against* Mangrove Palace! Was that all just to cover your tracks?"

"I was thinking about all of us! I mean, yeah, the construction could put the lemon shark nursery at risk, but there was no guarantee it would harm them. Not for sure. And think about what we'd gain! If that stock took off the way Maxwell said it would, we'd be able to sail the seas, researching sharks for the rest of our lives, worry-free! That was worth a small compromise, right?"

Cap looked at us like he was hoping we'd give him our wholehearted approval. What he got instead were two cold stares. I'd seen crooks tell themselves plenty of lies to justify their misdeeds, but all the rationalization in the world didn't make criminal behavior like Cap's okay.

"So in order to help sharks, you teamed up with a notorious shark hunter to kidnap a renowned shark advocate and inspired mass shark-hating hysteria by framing a shark for a crime it didn't commit, all so you could help pass a construction project that would endanger more sharks?" Joe asked. "A small compromise is settling for onion rings when you really want whale fries. I don't even know what you call that."

"It doesn't sound good when you put it that way," Cap murmured.

"You didn't help sharks," I said. "You betrayed them."

"I didn't!" he yelled, only to see our expressions and backpedal a second later. "Well, maybe some of them. The lemon sharks in the nursery might have been affected, but we could have used the profits from selling the stock to help so many more! We can't help any sharks if Shark Lab isn't out on the water conducting research. Trip said to trust her to come up with the money, like she always did, but I didn't see how she was going to save the day this time, and it was my boat she was asking me to risk. What choice did I have?"

"Maybe one that didn't involve multiple major crimes?" Joe suggested.

"It was only supposed to be for a day," he said, as if that made it any better. "The captains all talk, and Diamond knew about my trouble with the bank. He came to me with the whole plan worked out. All I had to do was convince Trip to change her vote, and then we'd let her go."

"And when she obviously didn't?" Joe asked, pointing up at the still-caged prisoner shaking the bars and glaring down at her ex-partner.

"Then I figured we'd just hold her for an extra day, until after the vote. I thought once it was a done deal and the stock became something with real value, then she'd have to see how much great work we could do by giving Mangrove Palace a chance. I mean, it was going to happen anyway at that point."

"But then your unwitting mayoral accomplice pulled a joker out of the deck by postponing the vote and playing the anti-shark card instead," I said.

"Sure sounds like a losing hand to me," Joe added.

"Me too," Diamond's voice growled from above.

All three of us flinched as the rogue captain stepped from the shadows with a speargun gripped in both hands. We flinched again as booming thunder shook the ancient lighthouse and the ceiling finally gave in to the storm's assault, sending rotting planks raining down around us. A flash of lightning exposed the wild look in Captain Diamond's eyes and made the sharks tattooed on his biceps shimmer like they were alive. Strands of long, wet hair clung to his face like sea snakes, and water dripped from his beard onto the bloody shark's tooth inked on his chest, making it look like it was bleeding for real. In that moment, amid the blasts of thunder and raining debris, I could have sworn we were under siege by a real-life pirate captain.

"Delaying that vote sure put a kink in my line," Diamond said. "No vote, the Tripster ain't cooperating, and now we got a lighthouse full of folks who know exactly what we done. I think it's time to cut bait on this whole operation."

"Trip still might come around and change her vote!" Cap pleaded.

Diamond shot a glance up at the shark cage. "What you think about that, Trip? You ready to vote yes on Mangrove Palace?"

Her voice was too hoarse to make out, but from the anger on her face and the way she was pounding the cage bars, whatever she was yelling wasn't the answer they were looking for.

"I'm gonna take that as a no," Diamond said. "Good thing we don't need her no more, anyway. Vote ain't gonna be postponed forever, and once she's gone for good, Maxwell's development will be approved just fine."

"That was never part of the plan!" Cap shouted.

"The plan was for you to play good cop, and me to play bad cop. Well, apparently your friend ain't impressed by cops at all, and I'm done playing."

Diamond shoved Cap against the wall and pushed past him to the gap in the staircase. "I'm gonna solve our little problem with Trip myself." He aimed the speargun at me and placed his finger on the trigger. "Right after I say goodbye to these two."

THE FINAL PLUNGE

16

JOE

TIME SEEMED TO FREEZE AS DIAMOND took aim.

Cap stood behind him, looking too stunned to speak. And then something changed.

"Nooo!" he screamed, grabbing hold of Diamond's arm just as he pulled the trigger.

The *twang* of the speargun firing was loud enough to hear over the storm. The spear flashed through the air and struck with a *thwack*. Frank and I turned to look at each other to make sure our eyes hadn't played tricks on us. Somehow, we were both hole-free! The lighthouse wall hadn't been so lucky.

A thin cord ran from the end of the spear back to the speargun. It was designed to keep the shooter attached to the fish so he could pull in his catch, only now it connected Diamond to the wall instead. The speargun was still gripped tightly in his hands as Cap tried to wrestle it away. Their faces shimmered with light from the lantern still looped around Cap's wrist. Both men were inches from the gap of open air where the staircase should have been.

The unloaded speargun wasn't doing Diamond much good at the moment, but that didn't mean I couldn't use it to my advantage. I grabbed hold of the cord tethering the speargun to Diamond's hands and yanked hard.

Captain Diamond must not have been used to his fish fighting back quite like this. My tug yanked him off-balance by only a few inches, and if he'd dropped the speargun right away or been just a little farther from the edge, he might have had a chance. His shriek echoed through the stormy lighthouse as he fell, the spear tearing out of the wall and falling after him.

Cap let go of Diamond just in time to save himself from the same fate. He was left standing at the edge of the last step, looking down at his falling former-enemy-turned-ally-turned-enemy-again. I couldn't see Diamond land, but I heard the splash.

The sound from below was joined by a crash from above. Joe and I watched in horror as a beam slammed into the top of EEE's shark-cage prison. Whatever was anchoring the chain holding up the cage had given way, and the whole setup started to plummet like an out-of-control elevator.

There was a sudden groan as the chain caught on something, snapping the cage to a stop just a few feet above Cap.

"Where is the pulley you used to raise it?" Frank hollered. "We need to try to stabilize the cage before it drops all the way down!"

The terror on Cap's face was easy to see in the next lightning flash. He looked down at the flooding ground floor.

"It's down there!" he called back, his voice wavering. "Underwater!"

"We can't just let her fall! There must be something we can do!" I shouted.

"I—I . . . I don't . . . I . . ." The lantern shook in Cap's hand as he trailed off. "What—what have I done?"

"Tell me where the pulley is!" I yelled. "I'm going to dive for it!"

Cap's expression turned from hopelessness to panic. "You can't dive into surging floodwater in the dark! There's debris everywhere! It's too dangerous! I can't have you hurt too because of me!"

"He couldn't have developed a conscience a couple hours ago?" I asked Frank, looking around frantically for anything else that might help.

I don't know if Trip heard us, but she must have realized hanging around waiting for a daring rescue while she was on the verge of plunging two stories inside a free-falling steel cage wasn't a great option. The diver-size opening at Trip's eye level hadn't done her any good as an escape route earlier when the shark cage was still secured to the ceiling, but now that the chain had given way, she didn't have any other choice. The cage was still too far from the wall for her to make a leap for the stairs, which left only one option. A ridiculously dangerous one. We watched as she climbed out through the opening and then clung precariously to the outside of the cage.

"She's going to try jumping into the water from up there!" I gasped.

"It's too shallow!" Cap hollered.

Trip looked down into the darkness. Even in the dim light cast by Cap's lantern, I could see the look of determination on her face. When the next thunderclap boomed, she nodded to herself and braced her legs against the bars. While she was taking deep breaths, I was holding mine.

"I think she's counting down from the thunder until the next lightning strike to give herself the best view," Frank guessed.

As soon as the next lightning flash arrived, she readied herself and was just about to leap when the situation shifted—literally! The roar of the waves below had become almost as loud as the thunder above, and the next wave to hit didn't just crash into the lighthouse. It nearly knocked it over! The entire structure seemed to moan as it tilted farther to the right, slamming us into the wall. Between the relentless battering of the storm and all the human-made ruckus inside, the condemned lighthouse was finally starting to collapse!

The shifting of the building had smashed the shark cage into the wall, raining shattered stone down on us. Trip barely managed to hang on to the outside of the cage without being thrown as it ricocheted off the wall. This time when the cage slowed, it was dangling only a few feet away from the spiral staircase above Cap, where the railing was still intact, close enough for her to jump!

She didn't hesitate for a second—and neither did the shark cage. She leaped from the edge at the same instant that the chain snapped, sending the now-empty prison cell plummeting the rest of the way without her. Trip grabbed hold of the rail and pulled herself over onto the stairs. As scared and tired as she must have been—I know I was!—she locked her eyes on Cap and marched right for him.

Cap must have realized that no amount of explaining was going to help his case. He scrambled for the window.

The storm had other ideas. Another massive wave crashed into the side of the lighthouse, smashing right through the boarded-up front door. The impact knocked Cap to his knees as the tide surged through the opening, filling the entire lower story.

Cap tried to get back to his feet and grab hold of the window ledge, but Trip got there first. Then she seized him by the back of his shirt and flung her traitorous friend off the stairs into the rising water.

Trip, Frank, and I all looked down to watch him disappear below the water's surface. But he wasn't under for long. With the front door no longer blocked, this time, when the wave retreated, most of the water retreated with it.

Cap and Diamond were left flopping around on the floor like fish ready for the dinner plate—or a jail cell.

Diamond was tangled up in an old fishing net, and Cap was grabbing his ankle like it might be broken. Neither of them would be getting off the hook this time.

Trip looked back across the gap in the stairs at Frank and me. "Welcome to Shark Lab, boys," she called, her voice low and raspy. "You're team members for life."

CATCH OF THE DAY

17

FRANK

THE STORM STARTED TO LET UP AFTER that. Trip crawled through the window while Joe and I took what was left of the stairs, and together the three of us were able to get our prisoners out of the lighthouse without anyone getting swept out to sea.

By the time dawn broke a couple of hours later, the ocean was calm again and the skies were clear.

We found Diamond's escape dinghy stashed in the channel not far from our paddleboards. Trip made one more run back to the lighthouse to reclaim her own board before we set out for town, picking up Boothby in the dinghy on the way. We paddled out side by side, leaving the ruins of Alligator Lighthouse in our wake, somehow still standing, but just barely.

Most of the fishing boats were getting a start on the day as the three of us paddled into the marina, hauling the catch of the day tied up in the dinghy behind us.

"Go figure," I told Joe and Trip. "We traveled to Florida to help a marine biologist save the sharks, and ended up helping save the marine biologist from human predators instead!"